**STRANGE AND DANGEROUS
PEOPLE, THEY HAD COME
TOGETHER AT THE TOP
OF THE WORLD. . . .**

A cynical pilot with too many pasts . . .
An alcoholic movie star with an uncertain future . . .
A beautiful con-woman with an eye for the finer things
in life . . .
An effeminate Englishman with a genius for death . . .

They all had their secrets.
Each of them wanted something.
And some of them were willing to kill for it in the
brutal country . . .

East of Desolation

JACK HIGGINS

East of Desolation

Jack Higgins

A DELL BOOK

Published by
Dell Publishing Co., Inc.
1 Dag Hammarskjold Plaza
New York, New York 10017

Dell ® TM 681510, Dell Publishing Co., Inc.

ISBN: 0-440-12447-6

Reprinted by arrangement with
Doubleday & Company, Inc.

Printed in the United States of America

First Dell printing—December 1982

For
Arnold Spector
—good friend

East of Desolation

CHAPTER ONE

I brought the plane in low over the sea and took her up to three thousand as land appeared and beyond, through the harsh white moonlight, the Greenland ice-cap gleamed like a string of pearls.

East from Cape Desolation the Julianehaab Bight was full of smoky mist indicating no wind to speak of and certainly nothing more than five knots, which was something. At least it gave me a chance of dropping into the valley at the head of the fjord. Not much of a one, but better than staying here.

It was cold in the cabin with the night wind streaming in through the splintered windscreen and the lighted dials on the instrument panel were confusing in their multiplicity, occasionally merging together in a meaningless blur.

And then, on the far side of the mist the waters of the fjord gleamed silvery white in the intense light and the strange twisted moonscape rolled towards the ice-cap, every feature etched razor-sharp.

It was time to go. I reduced speed, put the auto pilot in control and unbuckled my safety belt. When I turned, he was there as he always was, the head disembodied in the light from the instrument panel, eyes fixed, staring into eternity as he lolled back in the co-pilot's seat.

11

I moved into the darkness of the cabin and stumbled, falling to one knee, my outstretched hand touching the cold, ice-hard face of the other and panic seized me as it always did and it was as if I couldn't breathe as I lurched through the darkness and clawed at the quick release handles on the exit hatch.

It fell away into the night and I stepped into space without hesitation, aware of the intense cold, feeling strangely free. I seemed to somersault in slow motion and for a single moment saw the plane above me in the night drifting steadily eastwards like some dark ghost and then I reached for the ring to open my chute and it wasn't there and I gave one single despairing cry that was swept away into the night as I plunged into darkness.

*

I usually only got the dream when I was overtired or depressed, but it always left me in the same state— soaked in sweat and shaking like a leaf. I lay there looking up at the ceiling for a while, then flung aside the bedclothes and padded across to the window. When I rubbed the condensation away a fine morning greeted me.

I was flying out of Frederiksborg that year, God-thaab the capital having got just a little too civilised for comfort. It was a small place about two hundred miles below the Arctic Circle on the southwest coast. The population couldn't have been more than fifteen hundred, but during the short summer season it was artificially inflated by the influx of two or three hundred construction workers from Denmark who were engaged in building rather ugly three-storeyed blocks of concrete flats as part of the government development programme.

But Frederiksborg, like most places on the Greenland coast, still had the look of a raw pioneering town, the mushroom growth of some gold or silver strike. The roads were unsurfaced and most of the town was scattered over a peninsula of solid rock. The houses were made of wood and painted red, yellow and green, and because of the rock foundations everything went overhead and telephone and electric cables festooned the air from a forest of poles.

The harbour was half a mile away at the end of a rocky road beside the new canning factory and contained half a dozen fishing boats, a Catalina flying boat used by East Canada Airways for coastal traffic and my own Otter Amphibian which was parked on dry land at the head of the concrete slipway.

It was almost ten o'clock and I went into the bathroom and turned on the shower. There was a quick knock on the outside door and I wrapped a towel around my waist and returned to the bedroom.

Gudrid Rasmussen looked in. "You are ready for coffee, Mr. Martin?" she said in Danish.

She was a small, rather hippy girl of twenty-five or so, a Greenlander born and bred, mainly Danish by blood which showed in the fair hair plaited around her head, with just a touch of Eskimo in the high cheekbones and almond-shaped eyes. Most of the year she spent housekeeping for her grandfather on his sheep farm in Sandvig about a hundred miles down the coast, but during the summer she worked as a chambermaid at the hotel.

"Make it tea this morning, Gudrid," I said, "I'm feeling nostalgic."

She shook her head in reproof. "You look awful. Too much work is not good for a man."

Before I could reply the sound of an aeroplane en-

gine shattered the stillness of the morning and I went
to the window in time to see an Aermacchi flip neatly
in across the harbour and drop flaps to land on the airstrip beyond the canning factory.

"Here comes your boy friend."

"Arnie?" There was a touch of colour in her cheeks
as she crossed to the window. "Any girl is Arnie's girl,
Mr. Martin. I hold no special rights."

It would have been pointless to try and pretend otherwise and we stood there together for a moment in
silence watching the wheels come down beneath the
skis with which the Aermacchi was fitted.

"I thought he was going to take those off and put his
floats back on," I said.

"The skis?" She shrugged. "He got an extension of
his service contract with the American mining company
at Malamusk on the edge of the icecap. Up there the
only place to land is the snowfield."

His landing was good—not excellent, but then we all
have our off-days. The Aermacchi rolled along the airstrip and disappeared from view behind the canning
factory.

Gudrid smiled brightly. "I'll bring your tea while you
have a shower, then I'll order breakfast for you. I'll
change the bed later."

The door closed behind her and I went back into
the bathroom and got under the shower. It was nice
and hot and very relaxing and after a while my headache started to go, which was a good thing considering
that I had a two and a half hour flight ahead of me. I
pulled on an old silk dressing gown and went back into
the bedroom towelling my hair briskly. In my absence,
Gudrid had brought in a tray and the tea, when I
poured it, was scalding. I finished the first cup and was

pouring another when the door burst open and Arnie
Fassberg blew in.

He was about my height, which was a little under six
feet, but the resemblance stopped there. My hair was
dark, his so fair as to be almost white, his face open,
mine closed and saturnine. As yet he had not been used
by life or at least had been used kindly and his forehead
was as unlined as any child's. By birth an Icelander, he
had perhaps the most incredible appetite for women
that I have ever encountered, and like all Don Juans he
was an incurable romantic, falling in and out of love
with astounding frequency.

He presented a slightly theatrical figure in his fur-
lined boots and old flying jacket and he tossed a
canvas holdall into the corner and moved to the table.

"I thought you might have left. I've probably broken
all records from Søndre Strømfjord to get here."

"Any particular reason?"

He helped himself to tea using my cup. "You're
flying supplies out to that American film actor aren't
you?"

He was referring to Jack Desforge who'd arrived unexpectedly in Godthaab early in June in his motor yacht
Stella. Since then he'd been cruising the coast fishing
and hunting and I'd been flying out supplies to wherever he was at regular intervals.

"Why the interest?"

"I've got a passenger for you. She got off the midnight jet from Copenhagen at Søndre. Wanted me to
take her straight to Desforge, but I couldn't oblige.
Have to be at Malamusk by noon with some spare
parts they've had specially flown in from the States.
Where is he, by the way?"

"Somewhere north of Disko in the region of Narquassit as I last heard; looking for polar bear."

There was genuine astonishment on his face. "At this time of the year. You must be joking."

"About the only thing outside of a Tibetan yak that he's never laid low. You never know, he could hit lucky. I've seen bear up there myself in August before now."

"But not often, my friend. I wish him luck."

"This girl—what's her name?"

"Eytan—Ilana Eytan."

I raised my eyebrows. "Israeli?"

"I would have said English." He grinned. "Not that it matters—in any language she's a lot of woman."

"Good looking?"

He shook his head. "Ugly as sin and it doesn't matter a damn."

"A rare combination. I look forward to meeting her."

"She's having breakfast downstairs."

The door opened and Gudrid entered as I knew she would, her excuse the clean sheets she carried. Arnie swung round and advanced on her.

"Gudrid—sweetheart."

She side-stepped him neatly and dropped the sheets on the bed. "You can cut that out for a start."

He unzipped one of the pockets in his flying jacket and took out a roll of notes. "I got paid, angel. A thousand dollars on account. Where would we be without our American friends?"

"And how much of that will go across the card table at the Fredericsmut?" she said acidly.

He peeled off two hundred dollar bills and held out the rest of the money. "Save me from myself, Gudrid. Be my banker like always."

"What would be the point. You'll want it back again, tomorrow."

16

He grinned. "Put it in the bank then, in your name. Just so I can't get at it. I trust you."

And as usual, she was putty in his hands. "If you're sure you want me to."

"Would I ask if I didn't?" He patted her on the bottom. "I'd better come and see where you do put it, just in case you get knocked down in the street or anything."

I didn't need the wink he gave me over his shoulder as they went out to tell me what that meant. Poor Gudrid. Always on hand to keep him occupied in between affairs, never facing up to the hopelessness of the situation from her point of view. And yet in his own selfish way, he had a genuine affection for her and she did act as his banker on occasion which was probably the only reason he had any money at all.

But I had enough problems of my own without worrying too much about other people's and I finished dressing quickly and went downstairs.

*

As was only to be expected at that time in the morning, the restaurant was empty except for the girl sitting at a table in the bow window drinking coffee and looking out into the street. I could see at once what Arnie had meant, but he was wrong about one thing— she wasn't beautiful, not in any conventional sense, but she was far from ugly.

She had a strong Jewish face, if one can use that term these days without being called a racialist—a proud face with strong lines that might have been carved from stone. Full red lips, high cheekbones, hooded eyes—a face that was unashamedly sensual and the straight black hair that hung shoulder-length in a dark curtain was perfectly in keeping. No Ruth in any cornfield this, but a fierce, proud little queen. An Esther perhaps or even a Jezebel.

She looked up as I approached, her face calm, the dark eyes giving nothing away. I paused, hands in pockets.

"Miss Eytan? Joe Martin. I understand you want to see Jack Desforge. Mind if I ask why?"

She looked faintly surprised. "Does it matter?"

"It might to him."

I sat down opposite her and waved to the waiter in the kitchen entrance who immediately produced a whale steak from the hotplate and brought it across.

"Are you his keeper or something?" she said without the slightest touch of rancour in her voice.

"Let's put it this way. Jack has a great big sign out that says: DON'T DISTURB. I fly supplies to the *Stella* once a week and he not only pays me double—he pays me cash. Now I just love that kind of arrangement and I'd hate to see anything spoil it."

"Would it make any difference if I told you we were old friends?"

"Not particularly."

"Somehow I thought you might say that." She opened her handbag and took out a wallet that was surprisingly masculine in appearance. "How much do you charge to make the sort of flight you're doing this morning?"

"Five hundred krone."

"What's that American?"

"Call it a hundred and fifty dollars."

She extracted three notes and flipped them across the table. "Three hundred. That means I've paid in advance for the round trip if he doesn't want me to stay—satisfied?"

"Considering that I'll be getting paid twice, how

could I be otherwise?" I took out my wallet and put the notes away carefully. "We leave in forty minutes. The flight should take just over two hours if the wind is right."

"That's fine by me."

It was only when she stood up that I realised just how small she was—no more than five feet three or four. She was wearing an expensive tweed suit, nylon stockings and flat-heeled pigskin shoes.

"One more thing," I said. "You're dressed just fine for those long country weekends, but you'll need something different for where we're going."

"Rugged country?" she said. "Well that should make a change. So far I've found the whole thing just a little disappointing."

"They don't wear sealskin trousers any more if they can help it," I said, "and a whaleboat with a diesel motor is a damned sight handier in rough weather than a kayak, but if it's the rough outdoors you want, I think Disko should satisfy you."

"I can't wait," she said dryly. "Where can I change?"

"Use my room if you like. It's on the first floor— twenty-one. I'll finish here, then I've a few things to see to. I'll pick you up in half an hour."

She went out through the archway and spoke to the porter who hurried round to pick up the suitcase she selected from the stack that stood against the wall and she followed him across the hall to the stairs. At that distance there was something vaguely familiar about her, but I couldn't pin it down.

She walked well with a sort of general and total movement of the whole body and in one very quick moment, I wondered what she would be like in bed. But that would have been Arnie's reaction. He probably already had his campaign mapped out.

Suddenly angry with myself, I turned back to my steak, but it was already cold and I pushed it away and helped myself to coffee.

I think it was General Grant who said: War is hell. He should have added that women are worse. I sipped my coffee and stared out across the wide street towards the harbour where the Otter glinted scarlet and silver in the sunlight, but all I kept getting was a disturbing vision of Ilana Eytan crossing the hall and her damned skirt tightening as she mounted the stairs. It had been a long time since a woman bothered me as positively as that.

*

I borrowed the hotel Landrover and drove down to the harbour, mainly to get the met report from the harbourmaster's office. I'd refuelled the Otter on flying the night before so there was nothing to do there and at a crate of Scotch per week, Desforge had become such a valued customer of the Royal Greenland Trading Company that their local agent had supervised the loading of his supplies himself.

I drove back to the hotel and went upstairs. When I went into the bedroom there was no sign of the girl, but I could hear the shower going full blast so I went into the dressing room and started to change.

I was as far as my flying boots when the outside door opened and someone entered. As I got to my feet, Arnie called my name and I moved to the door. I was too late. By the time I reached the bedroom, he was already entering the bathroom. He backed out hurriedly and Ilana Eytan appeared a moment later swathed in a large white bath towel.

"I don't know what's supposed to be going on,"

she said. "But would you kindly send Little Boy Blue here about his business."

Arnie stood there speechless and she shut the door in his face. I tapped him on the shoulder. "On your way, Arnie."

"What a woman," he whispered. "My God, Joe, her breasts, her thighs—such perfection. I've never seen anything like it."

"Yes you have," I said. "About three thousand and forty-seven times." I pushed him out into the corridor and slammed the door.

I returned to the dressing room and pulled on a sweater and an old green kapok-filled parka with a fur-lined hood. When I went back into the bedroom Ilana Eytan was standing in front of the dressing table mirror combing her hair. She was wearing ski pants, cossack boots and a heavy Norwegian sweater.

"Arnie thought it was me in there," I said. "He didn't mean any harm."

"They never do."

There was a hip-length sheepskin jacket on the bed beside the open suitcase and as she picked it up and pulled it on, I once again had that strange feeling of familiarity.

"Haven't I seen you somewhere before?" I said and then the obvious possibility occurred to me. "In pictures maybe?"

She buttoned up the jacket, examined herself carefully in the mirror and put the comb to her hair again. "I've made a couple."

"With Jack?" And then I remembered. "Now I've got it. You played the Algerian girl in that last film of his. The film about gun-running."

"Go to the head of the class," she said brightly and zipped up her suitcase. "What did you think of it?"

21

"Wonderful," I said. "I don't know how he keeps it up. After all, he made his first film the year I was born."

"You make a poor liar," she said calmly. "That film was the original bomb. It sank without trace."

In spite of her apparent calmness there was a harsh, cutting edge to her voice that left me silent, but in any case she gave me no chance to reply and went out into the corridor leaving me to follow with her suitcase feeling strangely foolish.

CHAPTER TWO

As we roared out of the mouth of the fjord and climbed into the sun, I stamped on the right rudder and swung slowly north, flying parallel to the bold mountainous coast.

In the distance the icecap glinted in the morning sun and Ilana Eytan said, "The only thing I ever knew about Greenland before now was a line in a hymn they used to sing at morning assembly when I was a kid at school. From Greenland's icy mountains . . . Looking down on that lot I can see what they meant, but it still isn't quite as back of beyond as I expected. That hotel of yours in Frederiksborg even had central heating."

"Things are changing fast here now," I said. "The population's risen to sixty thousand since the war and the Danish government is putting a lot of money into development."

"Another thing, it isn't as cold as I thought it would be."

"It never is in the summer, particularly in the south-west. There's a lot of sheep farming down there, but things are still pretty primitive north of the Arctic Circle. Up around Disko you'll find plenty of Eskimos who still live the way they've always done."

"And that's where Jack is?"

I nodded. "Near the village called Narquassit as I

last heard. He's been looking for polar bear for the past couple of weeks."

"That sounds like Jack. How well have you got to know him since he's been up here?"

"Well enough."

She laughed abruptly, that strange harsh laugh of hers. "You look like the type he likes to tell his troubles to."

"And what type would that be?"

"What he fondly believes to be the rugged man of action. He's played bush pilot himself so many times in pictures over the years that he imagines he knows the real thing when he sees it."

"And I'm not it?"

"Nobody's real—not in Jack's terms. They couldn't be. He can never see beyond a neatly packaged hour and a half script." She lit a cigarette and leaned back in her seat. "I used to love the movies when I was a kid and then something happened. I don't know what it was, but one night when the hero and the girl got to- gether for the final clinch I suddenly wondered what they were going to do for the next forty-three years. When you begin thinking like that the whole house of cards comes tumbling down."

"Not for Jack," I said. "He's been living in a fantasy world for so long that reality has ceased to exist."

She turned, the narrow crease between her eyes a warning sign that I failed to notice. "And what's that supposed to mean?"

Considering the way she'd been talking I was more than a little surprised at her reaction. I shrugged. "He's playing a part right now, isn't he? The rugged ad- venturer cruising the Greenland coast? He'll spend the day in a dory helping to bait and hook a three-thou- sand-foot line or he'll go seal hunting amongst the pack ice in a kayak, but there's always the *Stella* to return to each night, a hot shower, a six-course dinner and a case of Scotch."

"A neat script," she said. "They could use you at Metro, but what about your own fantasy life?"

"I don't follow you."

"The tough bush pilot act, the flying boots, the fur-lined parka—the whole bit. Just who are you trying to kid? I wouldn't mind betting you even carry a gun."

"A .38 Smith and Wesson," I lied. "It's in the map compartment, but I haven't had time to shoot anyone lately."

I'd managed a nice bright reply, but she was hitting a bit too close for comfort and I think she knew it. For a little while I busied myself unnecessarily with a chart on my knee checking our course.

About five minutes later we came down through a cloud and she gave a sudden exclamation. "Look over there."

A quarter of a mile away, half a dozen three-masted schooners played follow-my-leader, sails full, a sight so lovely that it never failed to catch at the back of my throat.

"Portuguese," I said. "They've been crossing the Atlantic since before Columbus. After fishing the Grand Banks off Newfoundland in May and June they come up here to complete their catch. They still fish from dories with handlines."

"It's like something out of another age," she said, and there was genuine wonder in her voice.

Any further conversation was prevented by one of those sudden and startling changes in the weather for which the Greenland coast, even in summer, is so notorious. One moment a cloudless sky and crystal clear visibility and then, with astonishing rapidity, a cold front swept in from the icecap in a curtain of stinging rain and heavy mist.

It moved towards us in a grey wall and I eased back on the throttle and took the Otter down fast.

"Is it as bad as it looks?" Ilana Eytan asked calmly.

"It isn't good if that's what you mean."

I didn't need to look at my chart. In this kind of flying anything can happen and usually does. You only survive by knowing your boltholes and I ran for mine as fast as I could.

We skimmed the shoulder of a mountain and plunged into the fjord beyond as the first grey strands of mist curled along the tips of the wings. A final burst of power to level out in the descent and we dropped into the calm water with a splash. Mist closed in around us and I opened the side window and peered out as we taxied forward.

The tip of an old stone pier suddenly pushed out of the mist and I brought the Otter round, keeping well over to the right. A few moments later we saw the other end of the pier and the shore and I dropped the wheels beneath the floats and taxied up on to a narrow shingle beach. I turned off the master switch and silence enveloped us.

"Where are we?" she asked.

"A disused whaling station—Argamask. Like to take a look round?"

"Why not. How long will we be here?"

"Depends on the weather. One hour—two at the most. It'll disappear as unexpectedly as it came."

When I opened the door and jumped down she followed me so quickly that I didn't get the chance to offer her a hand down. It was colder than Frederiksborg, but still surprisingly mild considering we were twenty miles inside the Arctic Circle and she looked about her with obvious interest.

"Can we explore?"

"If you like."

We followed the beach and scrambled up an old concrete slipway that brought us to the shore-end of the pier. The mountain lifted above us shrouded in mist and the broken shell of the old whale-oil processing factory and the ruins of forty or fifty cottages crouched together at its foot.

It started to rain slightly as we walked along what had once been the main street and she pushed her hands into her pockets and laughed, a strange excitement in her voice.

"Now this I like—always have since I was a kid. Walking in the rain with the mist closing in."

"And keeping out the world," I said. "I know the feeling."

She turned and looked at me in some surprise, then laughed suddenly, but this time it lacked its usual harsh edge. She had changed. It was difficult to decide exactly how—just a general softening up, I suppose, but for the moment at any rate, she had become a different person.

"Welcome to the club. You said this was once a whaling station?"

I nodded. "Abandoned towards the end of the last century."

"What happened?"

"They simply ran out of whale in commercial quantities." I shrugged. "Most years there were four or five hundred ships up here. They over-fished, that was the trouble. Just like the buffalo—hunted to extinction."

There was a small ruined church at the end of the

street, a cemetery behind it enclosed by a broken wall and we went inside and paused at the first lichen covered headstone.

"Angus McClaren—died 1830," she said aloud. "A Scot."

I nodded. "That was a bad year in whaling history. The pack ice didn't break up as early as usual and nineteen British whalers were caught in it out there. They say there were more than a thousand men on the ice at one time."

She moved on reading the half-obliterated names aloud as she passed slowly amongst the graves. She paused at one stone, a slight frown on her face, then dropped to one knee and rubbed the green moss away with a gloved hand.

A Star of David appeared, carved with the same loving care that had distinguished the ornate Celtic crosses on the other stones and like them, the inscription was in English.

"Aaron Isaacs," she said as if to herself, her voice little more than a whisper. "Bosun—*Sea Queen* out of Liverpool. Killed by a whale at sea—27th July, 1863."

She knelt there staring at the inscription, a hand on the stone itself, sadness on her face and finding me standing over her, rose to her feet looking strangely embarrassed for a girl who normally seemed so cast-iron and for the first time, I wondered just how deep that surface toughness went.

She heaved herself up on top of a square stone tomb and sat on the edge, legs dangling. "I forgot my cigarettes. Can you oblige?"

I produced my old silver cigarette case and passed it up. She helped herself and paused before returning it, a slight frown on her face as she examined the lid.

"What's the crest?"

"Fleet Air Arm."

"Is that where you learned to fly?" I nodded and she shook her head. "The worst bit of casting I've seen in years. You're no more a bush pilot than my Uncle Max."

"Should I be flattered or otherwise?"

"Depends how you look at it. He's something in the City—a partner in one of the merchant banking houses I think. Some kind of finance anyway."

I smiled. "We don't all look like Humphrey Bogart you know or Jack Desforge for that matter."

"All right," she said. "Let's do it the hard way. Why Greenland? There must be other places."

"Simple—I can earn twice as much here in the four months of the summer season as I could in twelve months anywhere else."

"And that's important?"

"It is to me. I want to buy another couple of planes."

"That sounds ambitious for a start. To what end?"

"If I could start my own outfit in Newfoundland and Labrador I'd be a rich man inside five or six years."

"You sound pretty certain about that."

"I should be—I had eighteen months of it over there working for someone else, then six months free-lancing. The way Canada's expanding she'll be the richest country in the world inside twenty-five years, take my word for it."

She shook her head. "It still doesn't fit," she said and obviously decided to try another tack. "You look the sort of man who invariably has a good woman somewhere around in his life. What does she think about all this?"

"I haven't heard from that front lately," I said. "The last despatch was from her lawyers and distinctly cool."

"What did she want—money?"

I shook my head. "She could buy me those two planes and never notice it. No, she just wants her freedom. I'm expecting the good word any day now."

"You don't sound in any great pain."

"Dust and ashes a long, long time ago." I grinned. "Look, I'll put you out of your misery. Joe Martin, in three easy lessons. I did a degree in business administration at the London School of Economics and learned to fly with the University Air Squadron. I had to do a couple of years National Service when I finished, so I decided I might as well get something out of it and took a short service commission as a pilot with the old Fleet Air Arm. My wife was an actress when I first met her. Bit parts with the Bristol Old Vic. All very real and earnest."

"When did you get married?"

"When I came out of the service. Like your Uncle Max I took a job in the City, in my case Public Relations."

"Didn't it work out?"

"Very well indeed by normal standards." I frowned, trying to get the facts straight in my mind. It all seemed so unreal when you talked about it like this. "There were other things that went wrong. Someone discovered that Amy could sing and before we knew where we were she was making records. From then on it was one long programme of one-night stands and tours, personal appearances—that sort of thing."

"And you saw less and less of each other. An old story in show business."

"There seems to be a sort of gradual corruption about success—especially that kind. When you find that you can earn a thousand pounds a week, it's a short step to deciding there must be something wrong in a husband who can't make a tenth of that sum."

"So you decided to cut loose."

"There was a morning when I walked into my office, took one look at the desk and the pile of mail waiting for me and walked right out again. I spent my last thousand pounds on a conversion course and took a commercial pilot's licence."

"And here you are. Joe Martin—fly anywhere—do anything. Gun-running our speciality." She shook her head. "The dream of every bowler-hatted clerk travelling each day on the City line. When do you move on to Pago Pago?"

"That comes next year," I said. "But why should you have all the fun? Let's see what we can find out about Ilana Eytan. A Hebrew name as I remember, so for a start, you're Jewish."

It was like a match to dry grass and she flared up at once. "Israeli—I'm a *sabra*—Israeli born and bred."

It was there, of course, the chip the size of a Californian Redwood and explained a great deal. I quickly smoothed her ruffled feathers. "The most beautiful soldiers in the world, Israeli girls. Were you ever one?"

"Naturally—everyone must serve. My father is a lecturer in Ancient Languages at the University of Tel Aviv, but he saw active service in the Sinai campaign in 1956 and he was well into his fifties."

"What about this film business?"

"I did some theatre in Israel which led to a small film part, then someone offered me work in Italy. I played bit parts in several films there. That's where I met Jack. He was on location for a war picture. He not only took the lead—he also directed. Most of the money was his own too."

"And he gave you a part?"

"A small one, but I was the only woman in the picture so the critics had to say something."

31

"And then Hollywood?"

"Old hat. These days you do better in Europe."

Suddenly the mist dissolved like a magic curtain and behind her, the mountain reared up into a sky that seemed bluer than ever.

"Time to go," I said and held up my hands to catch her as she jumped down.

She looked up at the mountain. "Has it got a name?"

"Agsaussat," I said. "An Eskimo word. It means big with child."

She laughed harshly. "Well, that's Freudian if you like," she said and turned and led the way out through the gap in the wall.

Just like that she had changed again, back into the tough, brittle young woman I had first encountered in the dining room of the hotel at Frederiksborg, safe behind a hard protective shell that could only be penetrated if she wished, and I felt strangely depressed as I followed her.

CHAPTER THREE

Off the southern tip of Disko we came across another two Portuguese schooners moving along nicely in a light breeze, followed by a fleet of fourteen-foot dories, their yellow and green sails vivid in the bright sunlight.

We drifted across the rocky spine of the island and dropped into the channel beyond that separates it from the mainland. I took the Otter down, losing height rapidly and a few moments later found what I was looking for.

Narquassit was typical of most Eskimo fishing villages on that part of the coast. There were perhaps fifteen or sixteen gaily painted wooden houses strung out along the edge of the shore and two or three whaleboats and a dozen kayaks had been beached just above the high water mark.

The *Stella* was anchored about fifty yards off-shore, a slim and graceful looking ninety-foot diesel motor yacht, her steel hull painted dazzling white with a scarlet trim. When I banked, turning into the wind for my landing, someone came out of the wheelhouse and stood at the bridge rail looking up at us.

"Is that Jack?" she asked as we continued our turn. "I didn't get a good look."

I shook my head. "Olaf Sørensen—he's a Greenlander from Godthaab. Knows this coast like the back of his hand. Jack signed him on as pilot for the duration of the trip."

"Is he carrying his usual crew?"

"They all came with him if that's what you mean. An engineer, two deck hands and a cook—they're American. And then there's the steward—he's a Filipino."

"Tony Serafino?"

"That's him."

She was obviously pleased. "There's an old friend for a start."

I went in low once just to check the extent of the pack ice, but there was nothing to get excited about and I banked steeply and dropped her into the water without wasting any more time. I taxied towards the shore, let down the wheels and ran up on to dry land as the first of the village dogs arrived on the run. By the time I'd switched off the engine and opened the side door, the rest of them were there, forming a half-circle, stiff-legged and angry, howling their defiance.

A handful of Eskimo children appeared and drove them away in a hail of sticks and stones. The children clustered together and watched us, the brown Mongolian faces solemn and unsmiling, the heavy fur-lined parkas they wore exaggerating their bulk so that they looked like little old men and women.

"They don't look very friendly," Ilana Eytan commented.

"Try them with these." I produced a brown paper bag from my pocket.

She opened it and peered inside. "What are they?"

"Mint humbugs—never been known to fail."

But already the children were moving forward, their faces wreathed in smiles and she was swamped in a forest of waving arms as they swarmed around her.

34

I left her to it and went to the water's edge to meet the whaleboat from the *Stella* which was already half-way between the ship and the shore. One of the deck-hands was at the tiller and Sørensen stood in the prow, a line ready in his hands. As the man in the stern cut the engine, the whaleboat started to turn, drifting in on the waves and Sørensen threw the line. I caught it quickly, one foot in the shallows, and started to haul. Sørensen joined me and a moment later we had the whaleboat round and her stern beached.

He spoke good English, a legacy of fifteen years in the Canadian and British merchant marines and he used it to every available opportunity.

"I thought you might run into trouble when the mist came down."

"I put down at Argamask for an hour."

He nodded. "Nothing like knowing the coast. Who's the woman?"

"A friend of Desforge's or so she says."

"He didn't tell me he was expecting anyone."

"He isn't," I said simply.

"Like that, is it?" He frowned. "Desforge isn't going to like this, Joe."

I shrugged. "She's paid me in advance for the round trip. If he doesn't want her here she can come back with me tonight. I could drop her off at Søndre if she wants to make a connection for Europe or the States."

"That's okay by me as long as you think you can handle it. I've got troubles enough just keep the *Stella* in one piece."

I was surprised and showed it. "What's been going wrong?"

"It's Desforge," Sørensen said bitterly. "The man's quite mad. I've never known anyone so hell-bent on self-destruction."

35

"What's he been up to now?"

"We were up near Hagamut the other day looking for polar bear, his latest obsession, when we met some Eskimo hunters out after seal in their kayaks. Needless to say Desforge insisted on joining them. On the way back it seems he was out in front on his own when he came across an old bull walrus on the ice."

"And tried to take it alone?" I said incredulously.

"With a harpoon and on foot."

"What happened?"

"It knocked him down with its first rush and snapped the harpoon. Luckily one of the hunters from Hagamut came up fast and shot it before it could finish him off."

"And he wasn't hurt?"

"A few bruises, that's all. He laughed the whole thing off. He can go to hell his own way as far as I'm concerned, but I'm entitled to object when he puts all our lives at risk quite needlessly. There's been a lot of pack ice in the northern fjords this year—it really is dangerous—and yet he ordered me to take the *Stella* into the Kavangar Fjord because Eskimo hunters had reported traces of bear in that region. The ice was moving down so fast from the glacier that we were trapped for four hours. I thought we were never going to get out."

"Where is he now?"

"He left by kayak about two hours ago with a party of hunters from Narquassit. Apparently one of them sighted a bear yesterday afternoon in an inlet about three miles up the coast. He had to pay them in advance to get them to go with him. They think he's crazy."

Ilana Eytan managed to disentangle herself and joined us and I made the necessary introductions.

"Jack isn't here at the moment," I told her. "I think that under the circumstances I'd better go looking for him. You can wait on the *Stella*."

"Why can't I come with you?"

"I wouldn't if I were you. Apparently, he's finally caught up with that bear he's been chasing. No place for a woman, believe me."

"Fair enough," she said calmly. "I've never been exactly a devotee of Jack's great outdoors cult."

The deckhand was already transferring the stores from the Otter to the whaleboat and I turned to Sørensen. "I'll go out to the *Stella* with you and I'll take the whaleboat after you've unloaded her."

He nodded and went to help with the stores. Ilana Eytan chuckled. "Rather you than me."

"And what's that supposed to mean?"

"When Jack Desforge starts beating his chest wig it's time to run for cover. I'd remember that if I were you," she said and went down to the boat.

I thought about that for a while, then climbed inside the Otter, opened a compartment beneath the pilot's seat and pulled out a gun case. It contained a Winchester hunting rifle, a beautiful weapon which Desforge had loaned me the previous week. There was a box of cartridges in the map compartment and I loaded the magazine with infinite care. After all, there's nothing like being prepared for all eventualities and the girl was certainly right about one thing. Around Jack Desforge anything might happen and usually did.

*

The diesel engine gave the whaleboat a top speed of six or seven knots and I made good time after leaving the *Stella,* but a couple of miles further on the pack ice became more of a problem and every so often I had to cut the engine and stand on the stern seat to sort out a clear route through the maze of channels.

It was hard going for a while and reasonably hazardous because the ice kept lifting with the movements of the water, broken edges snapping together like the jaws of a steel trap. Twice I was almost caught and each time got clear only by boosting power at exactly the right moment. When I finally broke through into comparatively clear water and cut the engine, I was sweating and my hands trembled slightly—and yet I'd enjoyed every minute of it. I lit a cigarette and sat down in the stern for a short rest.

The wind that lifted off the water was cold, but the sun shone brightly in that eternal blue sky and the coastal scenery with the mountains and the icecap in the distance was incredibly beautiful—as spectacular as I'd seen anywhere.

Suddenly everything seemed to come together, the sea and the wind, the sun, the sky, the mountains and the icecap, fusing into a breathless moment of perfection in which the world seemed to stop. I floated there, hardly daring to breathe, waiting for a sign, if you like, but of what, I hadn't the remotest idea and then gradually it all came floating back, the touch of the wind on my face, the pack ice grinding upon itself, the harsh taste of the cigarette as the smoke caught at the back of my throat. One thing at least I had learned, perhaps hadn't faced up to before. There were other reasons for my presence on this wild and lovely coast than those I had given Ilana Eytan.

I started the engine again and moved on, and ten minutes later saw the tracer of blue smoke drifting into the air above a spine of rock that walled off the beach. I found the hunting party on the other side crouched round a fire of blazing driftwood, their kayaks drawn up on the beach. Desforge squatted with his back to me, a tin cup in one hand, a bottle in the other. At the sound of the whaleboat's engine he turned and, recognising me, let out a great roar of delight.

"Joe, baby, what's the good news?"

He came down the beach as I ran the whaleboat in through the broken ice and as always when we met, there was a slight edge of unreality to the whole thing for me; a sort of surprise to find that he actually existed in real life. The immense figure, the mane of brown hair and the face—that wonderful, craggy, used-up face that looked as if it had experienced everything life had to offer and had not been defeated. The face known the world over to millions of people even in the present version which included an untidy fringe of iron-grey beard and gave him—perhaps intentionally—an uncanny resemblance to Ernest Hemingway who I knew had always been a personal idol of his.

But how *was* one supposed to feel when confronted by a living legend? He'd made his first film at the age of sixteen in 1930, the year I was born. By 1939 he was almost rivalling Gable in popularity and a tour as a rear gunner in a B.17 bomber when America entered the Second World War made him a bigger draw than ever when he returned to make films during the forties and fifties.

But over the past few years one seemed to hear more and more about his personal life. As his film appearances decreased, he seemed to spend most of his time roaming the world in the *Stella* and the scandals increased by a sort of inverse ratio that still kept his name constantly before the public. A saloon brawl in London, a punch-up with Italian police in Rome, an unsavoury court case in the States involving a fifteen-year-old whose mother said he'd promised to marry the girl and still wanted him to.

These and a score of similar affairs had given him a sort of legendary notoriety that still made him an object of public veneration wherever he went and yet I knew from the things he had told me—usually after a bout of heavy drinking—that his career was virtually in ruins and that except for a part in a low budget French film, he hadn't worked in two years.

"You're just in time for the kill," he said. "These boys have finally managed to find a bear for me."

I slung the Winchester over my shoulder and jumped to the sand. "A small one I hope."

He frowned and nodded at the Winchester. "What in the hell do you want with that thing?"

"Protection," I said. "With you and your damned bear around I'm going to need all I can get."

There was a clump of harpoons standing in the wet sand beside the kayaks and he pulled one loose and brandished it fiercely.

"This is all you need; all any man needs. It's the only way—the only way with any truth or meaning."

Any minute now he was going to tell me just how noble death was and I cut in on him quickly and patted the Winchester.

"Well this is my way—the Joe Martin way. Any bear who comes within a hundred yards of me gets the whole magazine. I'm allergic to the smell of their fur."

He roared with laughter and slapped me on the back. "Joe, baby, you're the greatest thing since air-conditioning. Come and have a drink."

"Not for me, thanks," I said.

He had a head start anyway, that much was obvious, but I followed him to the fire and squatted beside him as he uncorked a nearly empty bottle and poured a generous measure into a tin cup. The hunters from Narquassit watched us impassively, a scattering of dogs crouched at their feet. Desforge shook his head in disgust.

"Look at them—what a bloody crew. I had to bribe them to get them this far." He swallowed some of his whisky. "But what can you expect? Look at their clothes—all store bought. Not a pair of sealskin pants amongst them."

He emptied the dregs of the bottle into his cup and I said, "I've brought a visitor to see you—a girl called Eytan."

He turned sharply, bewilderment on his face. "Ilana —here? You're kidding."

I shook my head. "She flew into Søndre from Copenhagen last night."

"Did she say what she wanted?"

I shook my head. "Maybe she's come to take you home."

"Not a chance." He laughed shortly. "I owe too many people too damned much on the outside. Greenland suits me just fine for the time being." He leaned across, full of drunken gravity. "I'll tell you something in confidence—confidence, mind you? There's a lulu coming up that'll put me right back up there on top of the heap and take care of my old age. Milt Gold of Horizon should be in touch with me any day now."

"Maybe this Eytan girl has a message for you," I suggested.

His face brightened. "Heh, you could have a point there."

There was a faint cry from along the beach and we turned to see an Eskimo trotting towards us waving excitedly. Everything else was forgotten as Desforge got to his feet and picked up a harpoon.

"This is it," he said. "Let's get moving."

He didn't even look to see if he was being followed

and I shouldered the Winchester and went after him, the hunters from Narquassit following. You can tell when an Eskimo is happy because sometimes he'll actually smile, but more often than not it's impossible to know how he's feeling at any given moment. Allowing for that I still got a definite impression that the men from Narquassit were something less than enthusiastic about the whole thing and I didn't blame them one little bit.

We reached the end of a long strip of shingle beach and started across a much rougher section that was a jumble of great boulders and broken ice when one of the hunters cried out sharply. They all came to a halt and there was a sudden frenzied outburst of voices as everyone seemed to start talking at once.

And then I saw it—a great shaggy mountain of dirty yellow fur ambling along the shoreline and as the first dog gave tongue, he paused and looked over his shoulder in a sort of amiable curiosity.

You don't need to be a great white hunter to shoot a polar bear. One thousand pounds of bone and muscle makes quite a target and it takes a lot to goad it into action, but when he moves, it's at anything up to twenty-five miles an hour and a sidelong swipe from one of those great paws is guaranteed to remove a man's face.

Desforge saw only the quarry he'd been seeking for so long and he gave a howl of triumph and started to run, harpoon at the trail, showing quite a turn of speed considering his age.

The dogs were well out in front, but the Eskimo hunters from Narquassit looked considerably more reluctant and I knew why. In their mythology and folklore the polar bear holds roughly the same position as does the wolf for the North American Indian, a creature

of mystery and magic with apparently all the cunning of
Man: on the other hand, they weren't keen on losing
their dogs and went after them fast and I brought up
the rear.

The bear loped across the strand and skidded on to
the pack ice, making for the nearest water, a dark hole
that was perhaps ten or twelve feet in diameter. He
plunged in and disappeared from view as the dogs went
after him closely followed by Desforge, the hunters
some little way behind.

I shouted a warning, but Desforge took no notice
and started across the ice to where the dogs ringed the
hole howling furiously. A moment later it happened—
one of the oldest tricks in the book. The bear sounded,
striking out furiously with both paws, erupting from
the water and falling across the thin ice with his whole
weight. A spider's web of cracks appeared that widened
into deep channels as he struck again.

The hunters had paused on the shore, calling to the
dogs to come back. Most of them managed it safely,
yelping like puppies, tails between their legs, but three
or four tumbled into the water to be smashed into
bloody pulp within seconds as the bear surged forward
again.

Desforge was no more than ten or twelve feet away
and he hurled the harpoon, losing his balance at the
same moment and slipping to one knee. It caught the
bear high up in the right side and he gave a roar like
distant thunder and reared up out of the broken ice,
smashing the haft of the harpoon with a single blow.

Desforge turned and started back, but he was too
late. Already a dark line was widening between him
and the shore and a moment later he was waist-deep
and floundering desperately in the soft slush. The bear
went after him like an express train.

Desforge was no more than four or five yards away from the shore as I burst through the line of hunters and raised the Winchester. There was time for just one shot and as the bear reared up above him I squeezed the trigger and the heavy bullet blew off the top of its head. It went down like a tower falling, blood and brains scattering across the ice and Desforge fell on to his hands and knees on the shore.

He lay there for a moment as the hunters rushed forward to catch the carcass before it went under the ice. When I dropped to one knee beside him he grinned up at me, the teeth very white in the iron-grey beard as he wiped blood away from his forehead with the back of one hand.

"I always did like to do my own stuntwork."

"A great script," I said. "What are you going to call the film—*Spawn of the North*?"

"We could have got some good footage there," he said seriously as I pulled him to his feet.

They hauled the bear on to the shore and the headman pulled out the broken shaft of Desforge's harpoon and came towards us. He spoke to me quickly in Eskimo and I translated for Desforge.

"He says that by rights the bear is yours."

"And how in the hell does he make that out?"

"The harpoon pierced a lung. He'd have died for sure."

"Well that's certainly good news. Presumably we'd have gone to the great hereafter together."

"They want to know if you'd like the skin."

"What would be the point? Some careless bastard seems to have ruined the head. Tell them they can have it."

I nodded to the headman who smiled with all the

delight of a child and called to his friends. They formed
a circle and shuffled round, arms linked, wailing in
chorus.

"Now what?" Desforge demanded.

"They're apologising to the bear for having killed
him."

His head went back and he laughed heartily, the
sound of it echoing flatly across the water. "If that
don't beat all. Come on, let's get out of here before I go
nuts or freeze to death or something," and he turned
and led the way back along the shore.

*

When we reached the whaleboat he got in and rum-
maged for a blanket in the stern locker while I pushed
off. By the time I'd clambered in after him and got the
engine started, he had the blanket round his shoulders
and was extracting the cork from a half-bottle of whisky
with his teeth.

"Looks as if they carry this with the iron rations,"
he said and held it out. "What about you?"

I shook my head. "We've been through all this before, Jack. I never use the stuff, remember?"

I had no way of knowing exactly how much whisky
he had put away by then, but it was obvious that he was
fast reaching a state where he would have difficulty in
remembering where he was and why, never mind make
any kind of sense out of past events. I knew the feeling
well. There had been a time when I spent too many
mornings in a grey fog wondering where I was—who I
was. At that point it's a long fast drop down unless you
have enough sense to turn before it's too late and take
that first fumbling step in the other direction.

"Sorry, I was forgetting," he said. "Now me—I'm

lucky. I've always been able to take it or leave it." He grinned, his teeth chattering slightly. "Mostly take it, mind you—one of life's great pleasures, like a good woman."

Just what was his definition of good was anybody's guess. He swallowed deeply, made a face and examined the label on the bottle. "Glen Fergus malt whisky. Never heard of it and I'm the original expert."

"Our finest local brew."

"They must have made it in a very old zinc bath. Last time I tasted anything like it was during Prohibition."

Not that he was going to let a little thing like that put him off and as I took the whaleboat out through the pack ice, he moved down to the prow. He sat there huddled in his blanket, the bottle clutched against his chest, staring up at the mountains and the icecap beyond as we skirted an iceberg that might have been carved from green glass. He spoke without turning round.

"Ilana—she's quite a girl, isn't she?"

"She has her points."

"And then some. I could tell you things about that baby that would make your hair stand up on end and dance. Miss Casting Couch of 1964." I was aware of a sudden vague resentment, the first stirrings of an anger that was as irrational as it was unexpected, but he carried straight on. "I gave her the first big break, you know."

I nodded. "She was telling me about that on the flight in. Some war picture you made in Italy."

He laughed out loud, lolling back against the bulwark as if he found the whole thing hilariously funny in retrospect. "The biggest mistake I ever made in my life, produced and directed by Jack Desforge. We live and we learn."

"Was it that bad?"

He was unable to contain his laughter. "A crate of last year's eggs couldn't have smelled any higher."

"What about Ilana?"

"Oh, she was fine." He shrugged. "No Bergman or anything like that, but she had other qualities. I knew that the first time I met her." He took another pull at the bottle. "I did everything for that girl. Clothes, grooming, even a new name—the whole bit."

I frowned. "You mean Ilana Eytan isn't her real name?"

"Is it hell," he said. "She needed a gimmick like everyone else, didn't she? I started out myself as Harry Wells of Tilman Falls, Wisconsin. When I first met Ilana she was plain Myra Grossman."

"And she isn't Israeli?"

"All part of the build-up. You know how it is. Israeli sounds better. It did to her anyway and that's the important thing. She's got a complex a mile wide. Her old man has a tailor's shop in some place called the Mile End Road in London. You ever heard of it?"

I nodded, fighting back an impulse to laugh out loud. "It's a funny old world, Jack, has that ever occurred to you?"

"Roughly five times a day for the last fifty-three years." He grinned. "I'm only admitting to forty-five of those remember." And then his mood seemed to change completely and he moved restlessly, pulling the blanket more closely about his shoulders. "I've been thinking. Did Ilana have anything for me?"

"Such as?"

"A letter maybe—something like that."

47

It was there in his voice quite suddenly, an anxiety he was unable to conceal and I shook my head. "Not that I know of, but why should she confide in me?"

He nodded and raised the bottle to his mouth again. It was cold now in spite of the sun and the perfect blue of the sky. A small wind lifted across the water and I noticed that the hands trembled slightly as they clutched the bottle. He sat there brooding for a while, looking his age for the first time since I'd known him and then quite unexpectedly, he laughed.

"You know that was really something back there—with the bear I mean. What a way to go. Real B picture stuff. We don't want it good, we want it by next Monday."

He took another swallow from the bottle which was by now half-empty and guffawed harshly. "I remember Ernie Hemingway saying something once about finishing like a man, standing up straight on your two hind legs and spitting right into the eye of the whole lousy universe." He swung round, half-drunk and more than a little aggressive. "And what do you think of that then, Joe, baby? What's the old world viewpoint on the weighty matter of life and death, or have you no statement to make at this time?"

"I've seen death if that's what you mean," I said. "It was always painful and usually ugly. Any kind of life is preferable to that."

"Is that a fact now?" He nodded gravely, a strange glazed expression in his eyes and said softly, "But what if there's nothing left?"

And then he leaned forward, the eyes starting from his head, saliva streaking his beard and cried hoarsely, "What have you got to say to that, eh?"

There was nothing I could say, nothing that would help the terrible despair in those eyes. For a long moment he crouched there in the bottom of the boat staring at me and then he turned and hurled the bottle high into the air and back towards the green iceberg. It bounced on a lower slope, flashed once like fire in the sunlight and was swallowed up.

CHAPTER FOUR

As we approached the *Stella,* Sørensen and Ilana Eytan came out of the wheelhouse and stood at the rail waiting for us. Desforge raised his arm in greeting and she waved.

"Ilana, baby, this is wonderful," he cried as we swung alongside and I tossed the end of the painter to Sørensen.

Desforge was up the ladder and over the rail in a matter of seconds and when I arrived she was tight in his arms looking smaller than ever in contrast to his great bulk.

And she had changed again. Her eyes sparkled and her cheeks were touched with fire. In some extraordinary manner she was alive in a way she simply had not been before. He lifted her in his two hands as easily as if she had been a child and kissed her.

"Angel, you look good enough to eat," he said as he put her down. "Let's you and me go below for a drink and you can tell me all the news from back home."

For the moment I was forgotten as they disappeared down the companionway and Sørensen said, "So she is staying?"

"Looks like it," I said.

"When do you want to start back?"

"There's no great rush. I'll refuel, then I'll have a shower and something to eat."

He nodded. "I'll get you the evening weather report on the radio from Søndre tower."

He went into the wheelhouse and I dropped back into the whaleboat, started the engine and turned towards the shore feeling slightly depressed as I remembered the expression in Ilana's eyes when Desforge had kissed her. Perhaps it was because I'd seen it once already that day when Gudrid Rasmussen had looked at Arnie, offering herself completely without saying a word, and I didn't like the implication.

God knows why. At that moment the only thing I could have said with any certainty was that in spite of her habitual aggressiveness, her harshness, I liked her. On the other hand if there was one thing I had learned from life up to and including that precise point in time, it was that nothing is ever quite as simple as it looks.

I thought about that for a while, rather glumly, and then the whaleboat grounded on the shingle and I got out and set to work.

*

I didn't see any sign of Desforge or the girl when I returned to the *Stella* and I went straight below to the cabin I'd been in the habit of using on previous visits. It had been cold working out there on the exposed beach with the wind coming in off the sea and I soaked the chill from my bones in a hot shower for ten or fifteen minutes, then got dressed again and went along to the main saloon.

Desforge was sitting at the bar alone reading a letter, a slight, fixed frown on his face. He still hadn't changed and the blanket he had wrapped around himself in the

51

whaleboat lay at the foot of the high stool as if it had slipped from his shoulder.

I hesitated in the doorway and he glanced up and saw me in the mirror behind the bar and swung round on the stool. "Come on in, Joe."

"So you got your letter," I said.

"Letter?" He stared at me blankly for a moment.

"The letter you were expecting from Milt Gold."

"Oh, this?" He held up the letter, then folded it and replaced it in its envelope. "Yes, Ilana delivered it by hand."

"Not bad news I hope."

"Not really—there's been a further delay in setting things up, that's all." He put the letter in his pocket and reached over the bar for a bottle. "Tell me, Joe, how much longer have we got before the winter sets in and pack ice becomes a big problem and so on."

"You mean up here around Disko?"

"No, I mean on the coast generally."

"That all depends." I shrugged. "Conditions fluctuate from year to year, but on the whole you're clear till the end of September."

He seemed genuinely astonished. "But that would give me another six or seven weeks. You're sure about that?"

"I should be—this is my third summer remember. August and September are the best months of the season. Highest mean temperatures, least problem with pack ice and so on."

"Well that's great," he said. "Milt thinks they should be ready to go by the end of September."

"Which means you can hang on here and keep your creditors at bay till then," I said.

"They'll sing a different tune when I'm working and the shekels start pouring in again." He seemed to have recovered all his old spirits and went behind the bar and poured himself another drink. "You flying back tonight, Joe?"

I nodded. "No choice, I've got two charter trips arranged for tomorrow already and there could be more when I get back."

"That's too bad. You'll stay over for dinner?"

"I don't see why not."

"Good—I'll settle up with you first, then I'll take a shower and change. How much is it this time?"

"Seven-fifty including the supplies."

He opened a small safe that stood under the bar and took out a plain black cash box. It was one of the strange and rather puzzling things about him, this insistence on paying cash on the barrel for everything. His financial position may have been pretty rotten everywhere else in the world, but on the Greenland coast he didn't owe a cent. He opened the box, took out a wad of notes that obviously contained several thousand dollars and peeled off eight hundred dollar bills.

"That should take care of it."

I fitted the notes into my wallet carefully and Desforge replaced the cash box in the safe. As he locked the steel door and straightened up again, Ilana Eytan came into the saloon.

I saw her first in the mirror behind the bar framed in the doorway and anywhere in the world from Cannes to Beverly Hills she would have had the heads turning.

She was wearing a slip of a dress in gold thread with tambour beading that must have set someone back a hundred guineas at least. The hemline was a good six inches above the knee, just right for swinging London that year and the black, shoulder-length hair contrasted superbly with the whole ensemble. Perhaps it was something to do with her smallness in spite of the gold high-heeled shoes, but she carried herself with a kind of superb arrogance tat seemed to say: Take me or leave me —I couldn't care less. I don't think I've ever met any woman who looked more capable of taking on the whole world if needs be.

Desforge went to meet her, arms outstretched. "What an entrance. I don't know where you got it, but that dress is a stroke of genius. You look like some great king's whore."

She smiled faintly. "That wasn't exactly the intention, but it will do for a start. What about the letter—good news? Milt didn't tell me much when I saw him."

"More delays I'm afraid." Desforge shrugged. "You should know the movie business by now. Milt thinks we'll be ready to go by the end of next month."

"And what are you going to do till then?"

"I might as well stay on here. It's the perfect solution under the circumstances and I'm having far too good a time to want to leave just yet." He turned and grinned at me. "Isn't that a fact, Joe?"

"Oh, he's having a ball all right," I assured her. "The only question is will he survive till the end of September."

Desforge chuckled. "Don't take any notice of Joe, angel. He's just a natural born pessimist. Give him a drink while I have a shower then we'll have something to eat."

The door closed behind him and she turned to look at me calmly, hand on hip, the scrap of dress outlining her body so perfectly that she might as well have had nothing on.

"You heard what the man said. Name your poison."

I helped myself to a cigarette from a box on the bar. "Jack's memory gets worse almost day-by-day. He knows perfectly well that I never use the stuff."

"That's a dent in the image for a start," she said and went behind the bar. "Sure you won't change your mind?"

I shook my head. "With a dress like that around I need a clear head."

"Is that suppoesd to be a compliment?"

"A statement of fact. On the other hand I've no objection to keeping you company with a stiff tomato juice."

"Well laced with Worcestershire Sauce?" I nodded.

"We aim to please. Coming right up."

There was an elaborate stereo record player in one corner and I moved across and selected a couple of old Sinatra LP's, mostly Cole Porter and Rodgers and Hart material, with one or two standards thrown in for good measure.

The maestro started to give out with "All the things you are" and I turned and went back to the bar. My tomato juice was waiting for me in a tall glass. It was ice-cold, obviously straight from the fridge and tasted fine. I swallowed half and she toasted me with an empty glass, picked up the bottle of vodka that stood at her elbow and poured some in. She added a scoop of crushed ice, something close to amusement in her eyes.

"The perfect drink. Tasteless, odourless, the same results as a shot in the arm and no headache in the morning."

I think I knew then what she had done and a moment later a sudden terrible spasm in the pit of my stomach confirmed it. I dropped the glass and clutched at the bar and her face seemed to crack wide open, the eyes widening in alarm.

"What is it? What's wrong?"

The taste started to rise into my mouth, foul as sewer water and I turned and ran for the door. I slipped and stumbled half-way up the companionway and was aware of her calling my name and then I was out into the cool evening air. I just managed to make the rail when the final nausea hit me and I dropped to my knees and was violently sick.

I hung there against the rail for a while, retching spasmodically, nothing left to come and finally managed to get some kind of control. When I got to my feet and turned she was standing a yard or two away looking strangely helpless, her face white, frightened.

"What did you put into the tomato juice—vodka?" I said wearily.

"I'm sorry." Her voice was almost inaudible. "I didn't mean any harm."

"What was I supposed to do, make a pass at you on one vodka?" I found a handkerchief, wiped my mouth and tossed it over the rail. "Something I omitted from the story of my life was the fact that I was once an alcoholic. That was as good a reason for my wife leaving me as all the romantic ones I gave you at Argamask. After I crawled back out of nowhere for the third time, she'd had enough. Her parting gift was to book me into a clinic that specialises in people like me. They did a very thorough job of aversion therapy with the aid of a couple of drugs called apomorphine and antabus. Just a taste of any kind of liquor these days and my guts turn inside out."

"I'm sorry," she said. "You'll never know how much."

"That's all right, Myra," I said. "You weren't to know. Part of that fantasy life of mine that we were discussing earlier today and I'm stuck with it. I suppose we all have things we don't care to discuss in mixed company."

She had gone very still from the moment that I had

used her real name and suddenly I felt bitterly angry and sorry for her, both at the same time.

I grabbed her by the arms and shook her furiously. "You stupid little bitch—just what are you trying to prove?"

She struck out at me and wrenched herself free with a strength that was surprising. I staggered back, almost missing my footing and she turned and disappeared down the companionway. There was a murmur of voices and a moment later, Desforge appeared.

"What in the hell is going on here?"

"A slight disagreement, that's all."

"Did you make a pass at her or something?"

I laughed. "You'll never know just how funny that is."

"But she was crying, Joe—I've never seen her do that before."

I frowned, trying to imagine her in tears and failed completely. Perhaps that other girl, the one in the graveyard at Argamask, but not Ilana Eytan.

"Look, Jack, anything she got she asked for."

He raised a hand quickly. "Okay, boy, I believe you. All the same, I think I'd better go and see what's wrong."

He went down the companionway and the door of the wheelhouse opened and Sørensen came out, his face impassive although I realised that he must have seen everything.

"I've got that met report for you from Søndre, Joe. Things look pretty steady for the next couple of hours, but there's a front moving in from the icecap. Heavy rain and squalls. You might just about beat it if you leave now."

It gave me a perfect out and I seized it with both hands. "I'd better get moving. No need to bother Desforge at the moment, I think he's got his hands full. Tell him I'll see him next week. If he wants me to come for the girl before then you can always radio in."

He nodded gravely. "I'll get the whaleboat ready for you."

I went below for my things and when I returned, one of the crew was waiting to take me ashore. He dropped me on the beach and started back to the *Stella* straight away and I got ready to leave.

I did the usual routine check then started the engine and ran the Otter down into the sea. I took up the wheels and taxied downwind slowly, leaning out of the side window and checking the water for ice floes before making my run.

When I was about a hundred yards north of the *Stella,* I started to turn into the wind and found the whaleboat bearing down on me, Desforge standing up in the prow waving furiously. I cut the engine and opened the side door as the whaleboat pulled in alongside. Desforge tossed me a canvas holdall, stepped on to the nearest float and hauled himself up into the cabin.

"I've got a sudden hankering to see some city life for a change—any objections?"

"You're the boss," I said. "But we'll have to get moving. I'm trying to beat some dirty weather into Frederiksborg."

The whaleboat was already turning away and I pressed down the starter switch and started to make the run. Twenty seconds later we drifted into the air and climbed steeply, banking over the *Stella* just as Ilana Eytan appeared from the companionway and stood looking up at us.

"What about her?" I said.

Desforge shrugged. "She'll be okay. I told Sørensen

to make tracks for Frederiksborg tonight. They'll be there by tomorrow afternoon."

He produced the inevitable hip flask, took a swallow and started to laugh. "I don't know what you did back there, but she was certainly in one hell of a temper when I went to her cabin."

"I'd have thought you'd have wanted to stay and console her," I said sourly.

"What that baby needs is time to cool off. I'm getting too old to have to fight for it. I'll wait till she's in the mood."

"What's she doing here anyway?" I said. "Don't tell me she just came to deliver that letter. There is such a thing as a postal service, even in Greenland."

"Oh, that's an easy one. She's hoping for the female lead in the picture I'm making." He grinned. "That's why I'm so sure she'll come round—they always do. She'll be sweetness and light when the *Stella* arrives tomorrow."

He leaned back in his seat, tilting the peak of his hunting cap down over his eyes and I sat there, hands steady on the wheel, thinking about Ilana Eytan, trying to imagine her selling herself, just for a role in a picture. But why not? After all, people sell themselves into one kind of slavery or another every day of the week.

Rain scattered across the windscreen in a fine spray and I frowned, all other thoughts driven from my mind at the prospect of that front moving in faster than they had realised at Søndre. I pulled back the stick and started to climb.

CHAPTER FIVE

Rain lashed against the glass in the hotel door, driven by a sudden flurry of wind and I turned and walked to the desk where Desforge was booking in.

"I'd say we just made it in time."

He grinned. "They can keep the great outdoors on a night like this. You'll have dinner with me?"

"I've one or two things to take care of first. I'll see you in about half an hour."

He went upstairs and I phoned through to the airstrip to see if they had any messages for me. There was one—an extra charter job for the following day. Nothing very exciting—a short hop of forty miles down the coast to Intusk with machine parts for the canning factory. I checked the flight time, made a note of it and turned away.

"Oh, Mr. Martin." The receptionist came out of her office quickly. "You've forgotten your mail."

She held out a couple of letters. One was a bill, I could tell as much without opening it. The other was postmarked London and carried the name and address of a firm of solicitors in Lincoln's Inn. There was a slight, hollow feeling at the pit of my stomach, but I slipped the letter into my pocket and managed a big smile.

"Thanks very much."

"And there was a message," the girl said. "A Mr. Vogel would like you to contact him."

"Vogel?" I frowned. "Never heard of him."

"I believe he booked into the hotel early this afternoon," she said. "I didn't see him myself."

I nodded. "All right—I'll attend to it."

Probably a wealthy tourist looking for some good hunting and prepared to pay through the nose for it. Not that I had any objections to that, but for the moment I had other things on my mind.

I think I must have sat on the edge of my bed staring down at that envelope for at least five minutes before I finally decided to open it. The letter inside was beautifully typed, short and very much to the point. It informed me that my wife had been awarded a decree nisi in the Chancery Court on the grounds of desertion, that she had decided to waive her right to any alimony and that a sum of two thousand, three hundred and seventy-five pounds, my share of the proceeds of the sale of a flat in the Cromwell Road, jointly owned, had been credited to my account in the City Branch of the Great Western Bank.

It was all very sad, but then the end of something always is and I sat there for a while remembering things as they had been once upon a time when the going was good and each day carried a new promise.

But even in that I was being consciously dishonest, forgetting quite deliberately the other side of the coin which had also been present from the beginning. Still, it was over now, the cord finally cut, and there was no bottle to reach for this time, could never be again. Let that be an end to it.

I didn't bother to change and simply took off my parka and flying boots and pulled on a pair of reindeer hide slippers. As I went out, Arnie Fassberg came up the stairs and turned along the corridor towards me, a bottle of schnapps in one hand.

"And what might you be up to?" I asked.

He grinned. "Gudrid's giving me a little supper in her room."

"What's wrong with your place?"

"She's on duty till one a.m. tonight. I couldn't wait that long."

He'd had a drink or two already, so much was obvious and swung me round like a schoolboy. "It's a great life, Joe. A wonderful life as long as you learn the big, big secret. Take whatever's going because you can never count on tomorrow."

At that moment the door behind him opened and a woman emerged. Arnie cannoned into her and her handbag went flying. She was strikingly beautiful and could have been anything between thirty and thirty-five, with the sad, haunted eyes of a Renaissance Madonna. He stood there gaping at her, that well-known expression on his face and she smiled suddenly, the sort of smile that comes easily to an attractive woman when she realises that the man before her is putty in her hands.

"I'm sorry," he said.

He dropped to one knee, reaching for the handbag at the same moment that she did and she almost lost her balance so that I had to catch her.

"Thank you," she said, glancing over her shoulder and then took her handbag gently from Arnie's hands as he stood there staring at her like a lovesick schoolboy. "Mine I think."

As she walked along the corridor, her shoulders were shaking with laughter.

"What a woman, Joe," Arnie breathed. "What a woman."

"Aren't they all, Arnie?" I said and left him standing there and went downstairs.

Desforge was already seated at a table in the far corner of the dining room and I moved towards him. The place was pretty full, mostly people I either knew personally or by sight, but there were three who were new to me—the woman from the corridor and two men who were seated together at the table in the bow window that Ilana Eytan had used that morning. I glanced at her briefly on my way across the room and sat on the other side of the table from Desforge.

He smiled. "You noticed her too?"

"Is there a man in the room who hasn't? Who is she?"

"I haven't had a chance to find out yet."

"You will, Jack, you will."

*

Desforge had a bottle of hock to himself and I shared a fresh salmon with him. We had reached the coffee stage when someone put a hand on my shoulder. I looked up and found one of the two men who had been sitting at the table by the window with the woman. I glanced across and saw that his companions had disappeared.

"Mr. Martin—Mr. Joe Martin?"

He was of medium height and thickset and wore a two-piece suit in thornproof tweed that had been cut by someone who knew what he was doing. His English was excellent with just the trace of an accent that hinted at something Germanic in his background although, as I learned later, he was Austrian.

I disliked him on sight and not for any particular reason. It was simply that I didn't care for solid middle-European looking gentlemen with bald heads and gold-capped teeth and large diamond rings on the little finger of the left hand.

I didn't bother getting up. "I'm Joe Martin—what can I do for you?"

"Vogel—Hans Vogel. My card."

It was an elegant strip of white pasteboard which announced that he was managing director of the London and Universal Insurance Company Ltd., with offices just off Berkley Square.

"What's it all about, Mr. Vogel?" I said. "This is Mr. Jack Desforge, by the way, a friend of mine."

"There is no need to introduce Mr. Desforge." He reached across to shake hands. "A very great honour, sir."

Desforge looked suitably modest and graciously waved him into one of the vacant chairs. Vogel sat down, took out his wallet and produced a scrap of paper which he passed across to me.

"Perhaps you would be good enough to read this."

It was a clipping from *The Times* only four days old and described an interview with the leaders of an Oxford University expedition which had just arrived back in London after successfully crossing the Greenland icecap from west to east. It seemed they had come across the wreckage of an aeroplane, a Heron, with a Canadian registration and a couple of bodies inside or what was left of them. Identification had been difficult, but according to the personal belongings and documentary evidence recovered, one was an Englishman called Gaunt and the other, a man named Harrison. The expedition had buried the remains and continued on its way.

Strange, but for the briefest of moments I seemed to see it lying there in the snowfield, the scarlet and blue of the crumpled fuselage vivid in the bright white light of the icecap. It was as if it had been biding its time, waiting for the moment when things were going well for me for the first time in years before drifting up from the darkness like some pale ghost to taunt me. *But why hadn't it burned?* With the amount of fuel left in the tanks it should have gone up like a torch.

I don't know how I managed to keep my hands still, but I did and read the cutting through again slowly to give myself time.

"What do you think, Mr. Martin?" Vogel's voice cut through to me.

I passed the cutting to Desforge. "Interesting, but hardly surprising. Earlier this year a similar expedition four hundred miles further north came across an American transport plane that disappeared on a flight from Thule three years ago."

"That seems incredible. Was no search mounted?"

"As a matter of fact, a highly intensive one, but a million and a quarter square miles of ice and snow is a hell of an area to cover." I was getting into my stride now, my voice strong and steady as I kept up the flow. "It happens all the time. It's the uncertain weather conditions on the icecap that do it. One moment a clear blue sky, fifteen minutes later the bottom's dropped out of the glass and you're in the centre of a raging storm and in a light aircraft that can be disastrous. What's your interest in this, anyway?"

"A large one, I'm afraid. My firm insured this plane, Mr. Martin. It disappeared more than a year ago on a flight from Grant Bay in Labrador."

"What was the destination?" Desforge asked.

"Ireland."

I raised my eyebrows. "Then they were more than a little off course. Who was flying?"

"Frankly, we don't know. The plane was owned by

Marvin Gaunt. Who this man Harrison was I haven't the slightest idea, but that's what it said on the name tab inside his jacket. There was also a wallet containing seven hundred dollars and an American Diner's Club card in the name of Harvey Stein. As a matter of interest, when we checked that through their London office it turned out to be forgery."

"Curiouser and curiouser," I said. "Just like Alice."

"The most puzzling thing is yet to come, Mr. Martin. The pilot for the flight as logged out of Grant Bay was a Canadian called Jack Kelso and the airport records definitely indicate that the plane only carried Gaunt and the pilot."

"Sounds like a good story line," Desforge put in.

Vogel said: "But one with little humour in it for my company. After the statutory period had elapsed we paid Gaunt's next of kin—his mother, as it happened—the sum of twenty-five thousand pounds called for under the terms of the insurance policy."

Desforge whistled softly. "I'd say that entitles you to some sort of explanation."

Vogel smiled thinly. "Exactly how we feel, Mr. Desforge. The whole affair is obviously far too mysterious. As I see it there are three questions which must be answered. Who was this man Harrison? What happened to Kelso? Why was the plane so far off course?"

Desforge grinned and emptied the last of the hock into his glass. "I said it was a good storyline."

Vogel ignored him. "As soon as I read the account of the find I contacted the Danish Embassy in London. They told me that eventually their civil aviation people would be inspecting the wreck, but that for various reasons there would probably be a considerable delay, perhaps even until next summer. Under the circumstances they obtained permission from the Ministry in Copenhagen for me to make a preliminary inspection myself."

"If you can get there," I said.

He smiled. "Which is where you come in, my friend. In Godthaab they told me that Joe Martin was the most experienced pilot on the coast." He took out his wallet and produced a typewritten document which he passed across. "That's the necessary clearing certificate from the Ministry."

I examined it briefly and passed it back. "Have you considered that there might be a logical explanation for this whole thing?"

There was something in his eyes for a moment, a greenish glow that appeared like some warning signal then faded.

"I'm afraid I don't understand," he said politely.

"That this Marvin Gaunt was up to no good, that Kelso never really existed at all, except for the specific reason of getting that plane out of Grant Bay. That he was really Harrison all along."

"That's good," Desforge said. "That's damned good."

Vogel sighed. "Ingenious, but unfortunately it won't wash, Mr. Martin."

"Why not?"

"Because Jack Kelso was most certainly flesh and blood and the London and Universal Insurance Co. has the best reasons for remembering the fact. You see under the terms of Marvin Gaunt's policy, the pilot was also covered for the same death benefit."

"And you paid out?" Desforge said.

"Twenty-five thousand pounds," Vogel nodded. "To Mrs. Sarah Kelso, his widow. She's waiting in the bar now with my associate. Perhaps you gentlemen would like to meet her?"

CHAPTER SIX

The crowd in the bar, although exclusively male, was reasonably well-behaved. There were one or two of the more prosperous locals, some Danish engineers and surveyors who were on the coast to work on government building projects during the short summer season, and a handful of young officers from a Danish Navy corvette that was doing survey work on the coast that year.

As we pushed our way through, Sarah Kelso was the subject of more than one conversation and I didn't blame them. Sitting there at a booth in the corner in the half light of the shaded lamp that stood on the table, she looked hauntingly beautiful.

Her companion stood up as we approached and Vogel introduced him first. "This is Ralph Stratton, an aviation expert from our Claims Department. I thought it might be a good idea to bring an expert along."

Stratton was tall and lean with a neatly clipped moustache and the look of a typical ex RAF type except for the eyes which had the same sort of shine that you get when light gleams on the edge of a cutthroat razor and which contrasted oddly with the slightly effeminate edge to his public school voice. He placed a hand as soft and boneless as any woman's briefly in mine and Vogel turned to Mrs. Kelso.

"I'd like you to meet Mr. Martin, my dear, the young man we were told about in Godthaab. I'm hoping he's going to help us."

"In a way Mr. Martin and I have already met," she said and held my hand for a long moment, the dark eyes full of anxiety. When she carried on, the soft, musical voice was charged with emotion. "I'm afraid the last three or four days have been something of a nightmare. None of this seems real at all."

There was a slight silence and Desforge said quietly, "Maybe I'd better see you later, Joe."

"Not at all," Vogel cut in quickly. "Mr. Jack Desforge, my dear. I'm sure you've no objection if he stays."

She stared up at Desforge in something close to bewilderment. "Now I know I'm dreaming."

He patted her hand gently. "Anything I can do—anything at all. You just name it."

She held his hand for even longer than she'd held mine—long enough to hook him good and hard, which was obvious from his face as we all sat down and Vogel snapped his fingers at a hovering waiter and ordered coffee. Desforge gave Sarah Kelso a cigarette and she leaned back against the padded wall of the booth, her eyes fixed on me.

"Mr. Vogel will have told you what all this is about, I suppose?"

"Except for one thing. I'm still not too clear why you should be here."

Vogel said: "I would have thought that was obvious, Mr. Martin. The whole point of our investigation is to determine the identity of the second man found in the wreck beyond reasonable doubt. Is he the mysterious Mr. Harrison, whoever he was—and that has yet to be determined—or Jack Kelso? It seems to me that Mrs. Kelso is the only person who can give an opinion on that point with any certainty."

"By going out there and viewing the body?" I said, and laughed out loud. "Considering Mrs. Kelso's vested interest in a positive identification, I must say you show a touching faith in human nature for a businessman, Mr. Vogel."

Surprisingly it was Desforge who reacted first. "That's a hell of a thing to say," he said angrily.

Sarah Kelso put a hand on his arm as if to hold him in check. "No, Mr. Desforge, your friend has made an obvious point. If that body is not my husband's then I am in a very difficult position. Mr. Vogel is well aware of that."

He leaned across the table and for a moment they might have been completely alone. "You know I'll do everything in my power to help you, my dear, but you must know also that my hands are tied."

She smiled gently and turned to me. "I have two young sons, Mr. Martin, did you know that?"

"No, I didn't, Mrs. Kelso."

"Then perhaps you'll realise now that there is more to this than the money—much more. I must know if that man out there is my husband. I must know. Can you understand that?"

The soft eyes were filled with anxiety, one hand reaching out in a kind of desperate appeal to touch mine gently. She was good—more than that. She was brilliant. For a moment she actually had me going along with her and I had to make a real effort to pull myself back to reality.

"Yes, I can understand that, Mrs. Kelso. I'm sorry."

"I had to inform Mrs. Kelso of what was going on," Vogel said. "She asked to come along and we were glad to have her. I should add that as well as a full physical description and photographs, she has also volunteered certain additional information as to identity which can only be confirmed on the spot. Under those circumstances I can't honestly see how she could get away with a deliberately false identification."

"Have you got a photograph with you?" I said.

He nodded to Stratton who produced a manilla file from a leather briefcase. He passed two photographs across. One was a straight portrait job in half-profile that looked as if it had been taken a year or two back and showed a reasonably handsome man in his late twenties with a strong jaw and a firm mouth. The other was more recent and showed him in flying gear standing beside a Piper Comanche. In the first picture he'd seemed pretty average, in this he looked like a man who'd decided that in the final analysis only the price tag was important.

I laid them down in front of Sarah Kelso. "So that's what he looked like?"

She stared at me, a slight puzzled frown on her face. "I don't understand."

"Let me tell you about the icecap, Mrs. Kelso. What it's really like up there. To start with it's so cold that flesh can't putrefy. That means that as soon as life leaves it, a body freezes so quickly that it's preserved indefinitely."

"But from the expedition report, I got the impression that the bodies were in an advanced state of decomposition," Vogel said quickly.

"There's only one thing living up there on top, Mr. Vogel," I said, "the Arctic Fox, and he's a scavenger as savage as any hyena."

I didn't need to elaborate. Sarah Kelso leaned back,

71

real pain on her face as she closed her eyes for a moment. Now she opened them and there was an astonishing strength in her voice.

"It doesn't matter, Mr. Martin. Nothing matters except the knowing."

There was another heavy silence broken by Desforge. "For God's sake, Joe, what's got into you?"

"I just wanted to make sure everyone had got the facts straight, that's all." I turned to Vogel. "Now we all know where we are, we can get down to business. First of all I'll have to know where the wreck is."

Stratton produced a map from the briefcase and spread it across the table. The position had been marked not as a meaningless dot but by two crossbearings that had been neatly pencilled in by someone who knew his job.

"Can you guarantee this is accurate?" I demanded.

Stratton nodded. "I drove over to Oxford myself just before we left and had a chat with the two men who led the expedition. They must have known their business or they wouldn't have got across surely?"

Which was fair enough. Only an expert navigator could chart a course with any certainty across that wilderness of snow and ice.

The route of the expedition had been plotted in red ink. It had started from old Olaf Rasmussen's place at Sandvig and had crossed the glacier at the head of Sandvig Fjord by the most direct route, following the high valley through the mountains beyond that led to the icecap. They had discovered the plane about a hundred miles inland not far from Lake Sule.

I studied the map for a while then shook my head.

"You're talking to the wrong man, Mr. Vogel."

He frowned. "I don't understand."

72

"It's simple. I fly an Otter amphibian, but I also have wheels which means I can put down on land or water, but not on snow."

"But what about this lake that's marked here," Stratton said. "Lake Sule. It can't be more than fifteen miles away from the wreck. Couldn't you put down there?"

"It's usually ice-free for about two weeks during September," I said. "Never any earlier than that within my experience."

"But you could take a look couldn't you? Tomorrow perhaps?" Vogel said. "I'll pay well. You'd have no worries on that score."

"I'd be taking your money to no purpose. I can tell you that now and in any case I've already contracted to make three charter flights tomorrow."

"Whatever you're getting paid, I'll double."

I shook my head. "No you won't. I'll still be here trying to make a living after you've gone and I wouldn't last long if I treated people like that."

"What about getting there by land?" Stratton said. "I see there's a road from Frederiksborg to Sandvig according to this map."

"A hundred mile cart track through the mountain. You could get to Sandvig by Landrover all right in five or six hours depending on weather conditions, but getting to Sandvig isn't the problem. I could fly you there inside an hour. It's what lies beyond that's the trouble. The glacier and the mountains and then the icecap. A hundred miles on foot over some of the worst country in the world. At a guess I'd say it took that Oxford expedition the best part of a fortnight." I shook my head. "The ideal solution would be a helicopter, but the nearest one of those to my knowledge is at the Ameri-

73

can base at Thule and that's a thousand miles up the coast from here."

There was another of those heavy silences and Vogel looked across at Stratton glumly. "It doesn't look too good, does it?"

Up until then I'd rather enjoyed myself pointing out the difficulties and making the whole thing look impossible, but there had to come a time when I offered the only obvious solution.

"Of course it's just possible that someone could put down in a ski plane up there."

Vogel was all attention. "Is there one available?"

I nodded. "A friend of mine runs an Aermacchi. An Icelander called Arnie Fassberg. You're in luck. He usually takes his skis off for the summer, but this year he's left them on because he has a regular charter contract with a mining company on the edge of the icecap at Malamusk."

"And you think he could land in the vicinity of the wreck?" Stratton said.

"He might with luck. It would really depend on whether he could find a snowfield."

"But not otherwise?"

I shook my head. "It's a nightmare world up there, a moonscape carved out of ice by the wind, cracked and fissured in a thousand places."

"This friend of yours, Fassberg I think you said his name was? He is here in Frederiksborg?" Vogel asked.

"He's based at the airstrip here. You could phone him through from the desk and leave a message for him. He'll get it first thing in the morning."

"Doesn't he live here at the hotel?"

"No, he has his own place on the edge of town."

"Perhaps we could see him tonight? I would like to get things settled as soon as possible."

I shook my head. "Tonight, he's otherwise engaged, Mr. Vogel, believe me."

"Which means a woman if I know Arnie," Desforge put in.

Vogel looked at me enquiringly and I nodded. "Something like that. He takes that side of life very seriously." I turned to Sarah Kelso. "You've already met, by the way, just before dinner outside your room."

Her eyes widened. "The handsome young man with the white hair? How interesting." Vogel frowned in puzzlement, but she didn't bother to explain. "If you don't mind I think I'll go to bed now. I'm very tired."

"But of course, my dear." His voice was instantly filled with concern. "I'll see you to your room."

"That isn't necessary."

"Nonsense, I insist. Time we were all in bed anyway. It's been a long day and tomorrow could be even longer."

We all stood and she held out her hand to me. "Thank you, Mr. Martin—thank you for all your help."

Desforge smiled down at her. "Don't forget now. If there's anything I can do—anything . . ."

"I'll remember." She smiled up at him warmly, the dark eyes shining for a moment, then walked away on Vogel's arm. Stratton said good night and followed them and Desforge and I sat down.

He sighed and shook his head. "There goes a real lady, Joe. I thought they'd gone out of style."

"You think so?"

"I know so." He frowned. "I don't know why, but you seem to be doing your level best to give her a hard time."

"She'll survive," I said.

Either he hadn't detected the acid in my voice or chose to ignore it, but he carried straight on as if I hadn't spoken. "She reminds me of someone I used to know a long time ago—Lilian Courtney. You ever heard of her, Joe?"

"I don't think so."

"She was one of the great original stars of the silent screen. Made her first picture before the first world war. She dropped out when talkies came in. It sounds crazy now, but she thought the whole thing was just a flash in the pan."

"I think I remember her now," I said. "Wasn't there some scandal concerning her death? Drugs or something?"

He flared up instantly. "That's a damned lie. There were always people who hated her—hated her for what she was—a lady. A real lady in a world of phonies."

He beckoned to the waiter and ordered whisky. "Strange, but the older you get, the more you start looking back and the harder you look, the more you realise what a game of chance the whole thing is. The right street corner at the right time."

"I'm with you there," I said. "What was yours?"

"The end of the pier in Santa Barbara in 1931—a fine rainy night with the fog rolling in. That's when I met Lilian. She'd gone out for a walk in the rain—one of her weaknesses as I discovered when I got to know her better. Some bum tried to get fresh with her."

"And you intervened?"

"That's it." He stared back into the past, a slight smile on his mouth. "I was just sixteen—a raw kid fresh from Wisconsin who wanted to act. She did everything for me. Clothes, grooming—even sent me to drama school for a while and, most important of all, she got me my first part in pictures."

"And what did you have to do in return?" I said. "Sit up and beg?"

It was a cruel and senseless remark that I regretted at once, but I got no chance to apologise. I wasn't even aware of his hand moving, but he had me by the throat with a strength I never knew he possessed and there was a fire in his eyes like hot coals as I started to choke.

"Not a thing—not a solitary damned thing. She treated me like a son. She was a lady, do you hear me? The last time I heard a man say a wrong word about her I broke his jaw."

He released me suddenly and I sucked in air. "I get the message. Sarah Kelso's the first lady you've met since?"

"She's got quality, that's for sure and it's a scarce commodity in the world we live in." He emptied his glass and shook his head. "What's it all about, Joe? Life, living, the whole bit. Ever ask yourself?"

"At a rough average I'd say around twenty-seven times a day."

"You can always see the funny side," he said, "I wish to hell I could." He stared sombrely into space. "I've been living on Stage 6 at Horizon Studios for so long that nothing seems real any more."

"Except Sarah Kelso?"

There was a cutting edge to my voice that I was unable to conceal and he was immediately aware of it and frowned. "What do you mean?"

"And the good Mr. Hans Vogel and his associate— the claims surveyor who can afford to wear eighty-guinea Savile Row suits. Salary scales in insurance offices must have risen considerably since I worked in the City."

"What are you getting at?" he demanded.

"I can smell fish as well as the next man and in this case you don't need to stand too close." He stared at me blankly. "It's shot full of holes, Jack, the whole tale. There are so many loose ends I wouldn't know where to start."

"Are you trying to tell me that Vogel's some kind of crook?"

Is anything ever that simple? I shook my head. "Maybe you're right, Jack. Perhaps you've been acting one part after another for so long that you've lost all touch with reality. Do you think the villain of the piece always has to look like Sydney Greenstreet or his bully boy like Bogart or Cagney?"

"Stratton?" he said incredulously. "You're trying to tell me that two-by-four is some kind of tough guy?"

"At a rough guess I'd say he'd slice your throat for a packet of cigarettes in the right circumstances."

He stared up at me, eyes wide. "Brother, do you need a good night's sleep."

"Which is just what I intend to get," I said sweetly and stood up. "See you around, Jack." And I turned and pushed my way through the crowd to the hall.

*

I didn't go to bed straight away, there was too much to think about. Outside the wind drove hail like lead bullets against the window and I lit a cigarette and lay on the bed with the radio playing.

When I first heard the knock I thought I was mistaken, it was so gentle, but it came again, a little louder this time and I crossed to the door and opened it.

Sarah Kelso smiled diffidently. "Could you spare me a minute?"

"My pleasure."

As I closed the door she moved to the window and

looked out into the darkness. "Is it always as rough as this?"

I crossed to the bed and turned down the radio. "I don't get the impression you came here to discuss the weather, Mrs. Kelso."

She turned, a wan smile on her face. "You're very direct, aren't you, Mr. Martin? In a way that makes it easier. You're quite right, of course. I didn't come here to discuss the weather. To tell you the truth I was hoping you might put me in touch with this pilot you mentioned—Arnie Fassberg I think you said his name was."

"You mean tonight?" I shook my head. "I thought I made it clear that he was otherwise engaged."

"Yes, I know," she said, a touch of impatience in her voice. "He's with some girl. Surely that doesn't mean I can't talk to him."

"What's Vogel think of this?"

"As far as I know he's in bed." She moved closer and said with a sort of quiet desperation that was very convincing, "I just want to talk to him, Mr. Martin. I want to know now, tonight, if he can help us. I can't stand much more of this uncertainty."

I frowned down at her, trying to work out what was going on behind that clear, pure mask she called a face, but she held my gaze unwaveringly.

"All right," I said. "Wait here and I'll see what I can do."

*

It was quiet at the end of the corridor and there was no sound from inside Gudrid's room. I glanced at my watch. It was just coming up to midnight and according to Arnie she was on duty till one a.m. When I tried the door it was locked, but as I started to turn away, Gudrid came down the service stairs holding a pile of blankets.

There was a glow to her skin and her eyes were shining, giving her the sort of look you find on the face of the cat that's had the cream. Whatever else you could say about him Arnie always seemed to give satisfaction.

"And what can I do for you?" she demanded brightly.

"I thought Arnie might be here."

"He left about an hour ago. He told me he wanted a good night's sleep for once. He's flying down to Itvak first thing in the morning. Was it something important?"

I shook my head. "It can wait. I'll see him tomorrow."

*

Sarah Kelso was standing at the window smoking one of my cigarettes when I went in and she turned sharply.

"Too late," I said. "He's gone home."

"Is it far?"

"Five or ten minutes walk."

"Would you take me?" She moved in close enough to fill my nostrils with her perfume and fixed me with those dark eyes of hers.

"No need to go overboard, Mrs. Kelso," I said. "You'll need boots and the warmest coat you've got. I'll meet you in the hall in five minutes."

She put a hand on my arm and said hesitatingly, "I was wondering—is there another way out?"

I nodded. "The service stairs take you right down to the basement. There's a door that opens into the backyard. Would you rather go that way?"

"It's just that Mr. Stratton went back down to the bar. If he saw me going out, he might wonder what was going on."

"It's certainly a thought," I said.

Just for a moment I'd caught her off balance and the eager smile slipped fractionally, but she obviously decided to let it go.

"I'll only be a moment," she said and went out.

*

There was a force eight gale blowing outside that drove the rain straight into our faces like rusty nails and Sarah Kelso held my arm tightly and huddled against me as we made our way along the main street.

We didn't talk because it took everything we had just to make progress, but when we turned into the narrow street that contained Arnie's place the tall wooden houses on our right broke the force of the wind and the going was a little easier.

Arnie's house was at the far end and backed by rising ground that rose into the foothills, a single-storey wooden building with a veranda at the front. There was a light at the window and a loose shutter swung to and fro in the wind.

I knocked at the door and after a while Arnie opened it and peered out. A scarf was knotted around his neck and he was wearing a dressing gown, but he didn't look as if he'd been roused from his bed.

In that first moment he only saw me and grinned. "Hey, Joe, you old devil. What can I do for you?"

I pulled Sarah Kelso out of the shadows and pushed her forward. "Mind if we come in, Arnie? It's damned cold out here."

His astonishment was plain, but he stood back at once so that we could enter. It was warm and inviting inside with a fire roaring in the stove so that the iron plate on top glowed cherry red.

81

Sarah Kelso took off her gloves and spread her hands to the warmth. "This is nice—this is very nice."

"Arnie Fassberg—Mrs. Sarah Kelso. We'd like to see you on a little matter of business, Arnie, if you can spare five minutes."

"Business?" he said and dragged his eyes away from her reluctantly. "I don't understand."

"Mrs. Kelso can do all the explaining necessary."

She turned and looked at me coolly. "You've been very kind, Mr. Martin, but I don't think there's any need for you to stay and go through all this again. I'm sure Mr. Fassberg can see me back to the hotel."

"Think you can manage that?" I asked Arnie who looked as if he'd been hit by a rather light truck.

"Oh, sure—sure I can, Joe," he said hurriedly. "You don't need to worry about Mrs. Kelso. I'll see she gets back to the hotel all right."

I'd reached the door when she called to me. When I turned, Arnie was helping her off with her coat. It was then that I noticed she'd changed into a peacock blue dress in jersey wool that buttoned down the front and finished just above the knee. The black leather cossack boots provided just the right final touch.

She crossed to me quickly and put a hand on my sleeve. "You won't mention this to Mr. Vogel if you see him, will you? I wouldn't like him to get the wrong idea."

"We must avoid that at all costs," I assured her solemnly. "You can rely on me."

Again that smile of hers slipped, but I turned and went out before she could say anything further.

The wind changed direction, roaring up the funnel of the narrow street, smacking me in the face with the force of a stiff right hand. I was bitterly cold and soaked to the skin as I turned the corner, but it didn't seem to matter one little bit. I wondered how Arnie was doing and laughed out loud. Whether he knew it or not, he was going to have to pay through the nose for whatever he got that night.

CHAPTER SEVEN

It was a fine bright morning as I walked up to the airstrip to check on the weather. Behind the town the mountains seemed very close in the crystal air like cutouts pasted on a blue backdrop and sheep drifted across the green foothills in a white cloud pushed by a shepherd and two barking dogs. On such a morning it was easy to understand how the country had got its name and for a moment I thought of those early Viking ships nosing into the fjords in search of the promised land.

Arnie's Aermacchi was already on the runway, a mechanic priming the engine while the young Icelander watched, white hair glinting in the sun. When he saw me he waved and crossed the tarmac, a big smile on his face.

"You look pleased with yourself," I said.

His smile widened. "She's quite a woman, Joe, believe me. Not as good as she thinks she is, but I certainly wouldn't kick her out of bed."

"I couldn't imagine you doing that to a seventy-five-year-old Eskimo woman. I suppose she found time to tell you the tale? Have you met Vogel yet?"

"As a matter of fact I had breakfast with him."

"Did you mention your night out with Mrs. Kelso?"

He spread his arms wide, an injured look on his face. "When did I ever open my mouth about a lady?"

"Don't make me answer that," I said. "What did she want to see you about anyway?"

He put a hand on my shoulder, his face serious.

"It's love, Joe, from that first wonderful moment when she bumped into me in the corridor outside her room. She just knew she had to come to me."

"I get the picture," I said. "It's bigger than both of you."

"That's it—that's it exactly."

"You lying bastard—how about the truth for a change?"

"That's just what I've given you. Oh, she wanted to know if I could help them with this other thing as well. The poor girl's obviously had a very bad time of it lately, but it was me she'd come to see."

"Then why all the mystery? Why did she ask me to shut up about it to Vogel?"

"I should have thought that was obvious. He's fallen in love with her and like most older men in that position, he's jealous and possessive. She doesn't want to get him stirred up, that's all."

"He never even loved his mother that one," I said. "Still, have it your own way. You're hiring out to Vogel then?"

"I can't afford not to at the prices he's offering. I'll be surprised if I earn my fee though. It's rough country up there. I can't think of anywhere off-hand where I could put down."

"There's always Lake Sule. Maybe you could land on the ice."

He nodded. "I thought of that, but I shouldn't imagine it would be firm enough. At this time of the year it's usually at the half-way stage. I hear you're going to Intusk this morning?"

"That's right."

85

"I was wondering whether you'd be interested in taking on an extra trip while you're in that region. I was supposed to fly a supply of drugs to the Portuguese fishing fleet's hospital ship. She's lying off-shore at Itvak. It's only another fifty miles."

"Suits me," I said, "as long as I get paid. What are you going to do?"

"I've got some supplies to deliver to the Royal Greenland Trading Company's store at Sandvig. I thought I could fly on from there and have a look at this plane wreck. It's the only way I can fit it in today. I've got a flight scheduled to Malamusk this afternoon and I can't afford to miss that."

I could understand how he felt. His connection with the Americans at Malamusk was too important to mess about with just for the sake of squeezing in a charter flight for someone he'd never heard of before. He had a seasonal contract. One trip a week with supplies and technical equipment that paid his expenses for the whole summer. Everything else was gravy.

"Are you taking Vogel and the company along?"

He shook his head. "I'm carrying too much weight on the Sandvig run as it is with those stores. Anyway this is only in the nature of a preliminary survey just to see if there is a snowfield in the vicinity. I don't think I'll have time to land even if I do find somewhere."

"All right," I said. "You'd better arrange for those drugs to be transferred to the Otter. I don't want to be late in getting off. I've a lot on today."

"They're already on board." He grinned. "You're always so reliable, Joe. See you tonight at the Fredericsmut."

I watched him run across to the Aermacchi and clamber in. He'd hardly got the door closed before the engine fired and he was away, lifting her far too soon.

His nose dropped, but he'd enough sense not to pull back on the stick until he had the power.

He roared across the harbour no more than twenty feet above the water and then his engine note deepened and he started to climb at just the right moment, banking into the sun, all for my benefit of course, nice and fast and showy and one of these days he was going to kill himself doing it.

*

I had a clear run down to Intusk and Itvak and was back in Frederiksborg before noon to pick up three passengers for Godthaab. From there I flew on to Søndre Strømfjord to meet the afternoon jet from Copenhagen. By four-thirty, I was on my way back with four young Danes who'd come to join the construction crew.

The weather had stayed perfect all day so that there had been no problems to speak of and yet I was tired—really tired. My arms ached and there was a gritty feeling beneath my eyelids as if I hadn't been getting enough sleep. What I really needed was a day off, not that there was any great hope of that.

When we reached Frederiksborg I circled the harbour a couple of times, just to check that I had a clear run, and noticed that the *Stella* had arrived safely. She was tied up at the main jetty and as I came in for my landing someone came out on deck and stood at the rail watching me. I was pretty sure it was Ilana Eytan, but at that distance I couldn't be certain.

I dropped the wheels and ran the Otter up the slipway out of the water. The young Danes gave me a hand to lash her down for the night and as we finished, a Landrover appeared to take them up to the construction camp headquarters. They offered me a lift, but I had business with the harbourmaster and let them go on without me.

When I came out of the harbourmaster's office, Arnie was down at the slipway sitting on a bollard beside the Otter smoking a cigarette and waving vigorously in the direction of the *Stella*. It was Ilana Eytan all right, standing there at the stern rail in her sheepskin coat and a red headscarf.

"I got the impression that your spare time was fully occupied at the moment," I said.

"I'd toss the whole damned lot of them out of the window for that one. What a woman."

"I seem to have heard that before somewhere."

He waved again and she turned and went below. "The story of my life."

"Don't give me that," I said. "Anyway, how did you get on?"

"At the scene of the crash?" He shook his head. "Not very well, I'm afraid. To start with I'd some difficulty in locating the plane. From what I could see it's lying at the bottom of a deep gully."

"And you couldn't land?"

"Out of the question. It's very rough country between there and Sule, Joe. There were one or two places that looked like vague possibilities, but I wouldn't dream of trying them without a ground check and that just isn't practical. I could break a ski or maybe my neck or lose the plane. Even the kind of money Vogel is offering isn't worth that risk."

"What about Lake Sule?"

He shrugged. "There was a hell of a lot of mist in that area so I didn't get down very low. From what I could see there was open water, but still plenty of ice about."

"So neither of us could land?"

"That's certainly the way it looked to me. You could maybe manage it in the Otter later in September, but I wouldn't give much for your chances at the moment."

"Have you told Vogel yet?"

"This afternoon. He was pretty upset about it, but as I told him, there just isn't anything more I can do." He glanced at his watch. "I'll have to go. I've got an evening flight to Malamusk—a special trip with spares for a drilling rig that's broken down. I should be back within a couple of hours. Will you be at the Fredericsmut tonight?"

"Very probably."

"I'll see you later then."

I started to refuel the Otter by hand from the stacked jerrycans at the top of the slipway and was still there when he took off ten minutes later. I watched him dwindle into the distance, a hand shading my eyes from the evening sun and when I turned, Ilana Eytan was at the top of the slipway.

"How's the intrepid aviator?"

I emptied the last jerrycan into the tank, screwed the cap home and climbed down. "Did you have a pleasant trip?"

"I've known better. We hit some ice on the way in this morning."

"Any damage?"

"The decks aren't awash if that's what you mean. Sørensen's taking her into drydock tomorrow."

"Have you seen Jack?"

She shook her head. "I think he's keeping out of the way."

There was a question I'd wanted to put to her, something that had been niggling away at the back of my mind. God knows why. She sat on the bollard Arnie had used and I gave her a cigarette.

"Will you tell me something if I ask it politely enough?"

"Try me."

"Why did you come? Why did you really come?"

She didn't seem particularly surprised. "Have you tried asking Jack?"

"As a matter of fact I have."

"And what was the verdict?"

"He says you're here to make sure of the female lead in his new picture."

"Well, now, that would seem to make a whole lot of sense to me." Was there a touch of irony in her voice? It was impossible to be sure and she turned up the collar of her sheepskin coat. "I can't really think of anything else that would bring me to a God-forsaken hole like this, can you?"

"Not off-hand, but I could give it some thought."

"You do that and in the meantime you can give me a hand to transfer my stuff from the *Stella*. Sørensen thinks I'd be better off in the hotel at the moment."

She turned without a word and started across the foreshore to the jetty. I stood there watching her go. She climbed to the concrete causeway, turned and looked down at me.

"Are you coming?"

"Are you sure you want me?" I said. "I've a feeling this could easily become a habit."

I caught her right off guard and for a moment, she was as tongue-tied as any young girl on a first date. Her recovery, when it came, was way below her usual acid standard.

"Don't be an idiot," she said uncertainly, turned and walked away.

But she knew when I started after her, I could tell by

the tilt of her head and the way her shoulders straightened and for some totally inexplicable reason—or at least that's what I tried to tell myself—my stomach went hollow with excitement.

CHAPTER EIGHT

Like most small communities in out of the way places Frederiksborg had very little crime, but we still had a policeman, Sergeant Olaf Simonsen, who was responsible for law and order in the town and an area as great as one of the larger English counties.

He was sitting at the hotel bar when I went in, having a beer with Jack Desforge, a tall, spare Greenlander, his skin weathered by forty Arctic winters to the semblance of puckered leather. Just now he was laughing at something Desforge had said, head thrown back, a quiet, kindly man, married with five daughters and very religious—a Moravian like most of the locals. And I had seen this same man with a look on his face like the wrath of God as he flushed out a bar full of brawling, drunken fishermen at the Fredericsmut on a Saturday night with the toe of his boot and an iron fist.

I sat on the stool next to him. "Hello, Olaf, what have you been doing with yourself for the past few days?"

He shook hands. "I had to go inland—the other side of the glacier at the head of the Stavanger Fjord."

"Trouble?"

"The usual thing—reindeer hunters at each other's throats."

"Anyone hurt?"

"A knifing or two—nothing serious. I think I've quietened them down. You know Mr. Desforge, of course. He's been making me laugh."

I looked across at Jack. "Anything I should know?"

"I've really hit the big time at last," he said. "Some guy turned up at the hotel earlier wanting an interview for the local press. Naturally I gave him one—I've never turned down free publicity yet."

"Which paper?"

He started to laugh again. "That's the whole point."

I turned to Sinonsen. "The *Atuagagdliutit*?"

He nodded. "I've just been explaining to Mr. Desforge—he's now immortalised in the pages of the only newspaper in the world that's published in Eskimo."

"And if that isn't worth another drink, I don't know what is," Desforge said.

Simonsen shook his head. "Not for me. I'll have to be off in a moment. I was hoping to catch you tonight, Joe. When I returned there was a memo from headquarters in Godthaab about this plane the Oxford expedition came across. Apparently a Mr. Vogel of the London and Universal Insurance Company approached them with a certificate of search from the Ministry in Copenhagen. I understand they recommended him to see you."

"That's right." I gave him the whole story, including the substance of the conversation I'd just had with Arnie Fassberg and he listened gravely.

"I can't say I'm surprised Arnie couldn't find a suitable place to land on skis up there, but if that mist had cleared a little allowing him a good look at Lake Sule he'd have seen that there was ample open water for a floatplane landing."

"Are you certain about that?"

He produced a piece of paper from one of his tunic

93

pockets and passed it across. "See for yourself—that's an extract from the weekly regional met forecast put out by the Americans from Thule. It indicates that mean temperatures have been higher than usual up there for the time of the year."

I had a look at the report which confirmed what he had said in slightly more technical language and handed it back. "That seems fair enough to me. They're usually pretty accurate."

"They have to be." He put the report back in his pocket. "So there's no reason now why you can't make the trip. What about tomorrow?"

I stalled for time. "What are you—Vogel's agent or something?"

He smiled. "I haven't even met him yet. This is official business now, Joe. The powers-that-be have decided I should go along to keep an eye on things generally and compile a preliminary report for the Ministry people in Copenhagen. It's unlikely they'll be able to get anyone out there till next year. In fact if my report is satisfactory, especially when considered in conjunction with the findings of this aviation expert Vogel has with him, they may decide to take it no further."

I wondered how Vogel was going to like having a policeman breathing down his neck, but only for a moment. I had my own problems. So I had been right all along. It had been waiting for me out there on the icecap for more than a year now and there was no escape. For a brief moment I saw it again in my mind's eyes, silver and blue against the eternal whiteness and a strange fatalism gripped me. I was caught up in a tide of events too strong to fight against and must go with the current and see what happened.

"I suppose I could manage that. It would mean altering my schedules for the next couple of days, but there isn't anything so desperately important that it can't be postponed."

"Good—I think an early start is indicated. Can you be ready for seven a.m.?"

"Any time you like. Will you see Vogel or shall I?"

"I'll handle that—it will give me a chance to meet him."

"A minor failing of mine," I said. "I like to know everything. That wreck is about ten miles east of Sule. How do we get there?"

"On skis of course. We'll do it in two or three hours."

"That's all right for you and me, but what about the others. Maybe they can't ski."

"Then they must learn," he said simply.

"And the woman?"

He shrugged. "All right, the woman we can haul on a light sledge, but the other two will have to ski or go on foot and they'll find it a rough walk, believe me."

"All right, you're the boss."

He adjusted his uniform cap to the regulation angle in the mirror behind the bar. "If necessary I'll come back to you later. Where will you be?"

"I'd thought of having a meal at the Fredericsmut for a change. It's some time since I've been there."

"The Fredericsmut? You may be in for a lively night, I warn you. There's a Portuguese schooner due."

I nodded. "I saw her entering the fjord on my way in. Who is it? Anyone I know?"

"Da Gama." He chuckled grimly. "I'd eat here to-night if I were you."

He went out and Desforge said, "And who in the hell is this Da Gama—Frankenstein?"

"Something like that. He comes in for supplies about

once a month and there's always trouble. One of these days he'll kill somebody—probably has already if the truth's known."

"Sounds like fun," Desforge said. "I think I'll come with you. I could do with a little action and it'll get me out of the way. I don't want to run into Ilana till I'm good and ready."

"All right," I said. "I've one or two things to do. I'll be back in fifteen minutes."

I left him there at the bar, went to the reception desk and phoned through to the airstrip. I explained that I wouldn't be available for the next couple of days, stressing that I was on government business and asked them to contact the people concerned in Godthaab and Søndre to suggest that they either rearrange their schedules or make other arrangements.

As I had anticipated, there was no particular difficulty and I went up to my room, stripped off my flying gear and had a quick shower. I'd just pulled a heavy Norwegian sweater over my head when there was a knock at the door. I opened it and found Ilana Eytan standing outside.

"I'm looking for Jack. Any idea where he might be?"

I lied cheerfully. "Not right now," and then for some perverse reason decided to go further. "I can tell you where he'll be later, though. The Fredericsmut—that's a place at the other end of the main street from here."

"I'll see him there then."

I shook my head. "I wouldn't if I were you. Rough fishermen, hard liquor and a roomful of smoke—not for little girls."

"In a pig's eye, Joe Martin," she said and went back along the corridor to her room.

*

The Fredericsmut was definitely for the lower orders, the sort of place you'll find in any town in the world from Singapore to Jackson Falls, Wyoming. In this case it was a two-storeyed wooden building with a veranda at the front. What went on upstairs was anybody's guess, but through the swing doors that opened from the veranda was a large square room where you could find good plain food in large quantities, any kind of liquor you cared to name and broadminded women. The one incongruity was a large and shiny juke box that stood by the door and never seemed to stop playing.

We sat at a table at the back of the room close to the bar and I ordered steak and chips for both of us and a lager for Desforge. The juke box was going full blast surrounded by a crowd of youthful Greenlanders, some of them shaking away to the manner born.

Jack groaned as if in pain. "Is nothing sacred? I come north looking for polar bear, the eternal struggle of man in an alien land, harpoons and sealskin trousers and what do I get?"

"Corduroy trews and the Beatles."

"Next thing you know one of those outfits in Carnaby Street will be opening up a branch."

I shook my head. "Just let them try and see what the Royal Greenland Trading Company have to say about it. Maybe they don't have a monopoly any longer, but they still swing a pretty big axe."

The crowd was building up now—construction workers looking for a little fun after a twelve-hour day, inshore fishermen, professional hunters, Danes and Icelanders with a few Norwegians thrown in for good luck, and Greenlanders, some looking pure Scandinavian, others a hundred per cent Eskimo and most of them falling somewhere in between.

"You know when I was a kid my old man was pretty strict with us," Jack said as we sat there waiting for the food to arrive. "He died when I was seven and the family had to split up. I went to live with my Aunt Clara in Wisconsin."

"Did you get on all right with her?"

"Couldn't have been better. She started taking me to the movies, something my father never allowed. This was in the silent days mind you. I can remember one old three-reeler I saw, *The Spoilers*. It's been remade three or four times. The version I saw starred Noah Beery and Milton Sills and they had one hell of a brawl on a set that looked just like this place. Funny how your memory works. I haven't thought of that for years."

An impudent looking young Eskimo girl in a black silk dress that was a size too small brought the food, leaning so close to Desforge when she put his plate on the table that her breast was crushed against his shoulder.

He asked her to bring him a bottle of whisky from the bar and she ogled him shamelessly, fluttering false eyelashes that somehow looked obscene fringing the slanting, almond-shaped eyes. As she moved through the crowd to the bar someone slapped her backside and there was a sudden burst of laughter. She didn't show the slightest objection when a bearded fisherman in an oilskin jacket pulled her close, kissed her, then passed her on to the man next to him.

"You know there are times when I feel like throwing up," Desforge said. "To think of a once proud people reduced to that."

"It's unfortunate, but primitive races seem to acquire all the vices of our kind of civilisation," I said, "never its virtues."

98

He nodded. "I've seen the same thing back home on Sioux Indian reservations. A great people reduced to putting on a circus act for tourists."

"There'll be nowhere left soon."

"I suppose not." There was an expression of settled gloom on his face. The girl brought the bottle and a couple of glasses and he poured himself a large whisky. "I've been thinking of doing a little reindeer hunting. I thought it might be a good opportunity while the *Stella* is in drydock."

"Got any ideas about where to go?"

"The barman at the hotel suggested Sandvig. It seems there are still a few of the old Viking settlements on view in that region or what's left of them. Sounds as if it would be worth the trip even if the hunting doesn't turn out to be a success."

"You could do worse," I said. "There's a man down there I'd love you to meet—Olaf Rasmussen."

"Rasmussen? Is he anything to do with Gudrid, the chambermaid at the hotel?"

"Her grandfather. He's about seventy-five, a real old Viking. Has a farm near Sandvig with eight hundred head of sheep, but he spends most of his time on excavation work on the old settlements on his land."

"Do you think he'd put me up for a few days?"

"No question of it—hospitality is his second name. Are you trying to run out on Ilana again by any chance?"

"No, not this time. I'll take her with me if she'll come. How do I get there?"

"That's up to you. You could charter Arnie if he's available or you could even squeeze in with us in the morning if you can be on the slipway at seven. We'll be calling at Sandvig on the way."

99

"I'd forgotten such a time existed," he said. "Still, it's a thought."

Just then I noticed Vogel, Ralph Stratton and Sarah Kelso standing just inside the doorway. Vogel saw me in the same moment and said something to the others. He was smiling as they came across.

"I've had a most interesting chat with Sergeant Simonsen, Mr. Martin. It would seem there is a chance for us after all."

"That still depends on what we find when we get there," I said as they seated themselves. "Even if a landing is possible on the lake itself, the weather has to be right. Earlier today for example, when Arnie Fassberg was there, there was such a heavy mist that he didn't get a close look at the lake at all."

"Is that sort of thing usual?" Stratton asked.

I nodded. "It happens all the time, even in summer. Hail, rain, mist or perhaps a blizzard that seems to sweep in out of nowhere. An hour later the sky is so blue that you can't believe it's real. How's your skiing, by the way?"

"I was born and raised in the Austrian Tyrol," Vogel said, "which means I was going to school on skis from the age of five. Mr. Stratton tells me his own experience has been confined to a couple of winter holidays in France, but I'm sure that should prove more than adequate."

"I'm the odd man out I'm afraid," Sarah Kelso said, "but Sergeant Simonsen seems to think that's no problem."

"From what I've heard you're going to get the de luxe treatment," Desforge assured her. "You'll arrive in style without a hair out of place. Now what about a drink?"

By now things had begun to get pretty noisy. People

crowded on to the tiny dance floor, there were occasional shrieks from the darker corners and now and then the sound of breaking glass echoed through the haze of tobacco smoke.

"This is hardly the London Hilton." Desforge leaned across to Sarah Kelso. "Are you sure you wouldn't rather go some place else?"

"Oh, I should imagine I've got pretty good protection," she told him. "To tell you the truth, I'm rather enjoying myself."

A moment later the doors seemed to burst inwards and Da Gama arrived. He paused inside the door, half a dozen of his crew at his back, a giant of a man in a reefer coat, an old cloth cap pulled down over his dark and greasy hair. He had tiny pig's eyes above flat cheekbones and his skin was so dark that I always suspected he had coloured blood in him.

The juke box kept on playing, but for a moment there was a lull in the general conversation. Da Gama said something over his shoulder to one of his men and laughed harshly. For some reason that seemed to break the tension and people started talking again. He moved to the bar, taking the shortest route, cutting straight through the middle of the crowded dance floor and anyone in his way got out of it quick.

Desforge emptied his glass and filled it again. "So that's Da Gama? From the look of him I'd say he's probably got a brain the size of a pea."

"It's his hands you've got to watch," I said. "He could break an arm as easily as a rotten stick."

Strangely enough it was Stratton who reacted most. His face had gone very white and there was a strange glitter in his eyes and then I noticed that his hands were resting lightly on the edge of the table and that he still had his gloves on. They were an expensive-looking pair in soft black leather and somehow deadly. I suddenly knew beyond any doubt that my first estimate of the man had not been far wrong. Effeminate perhaps, but not soft, a mistake people often made about homosexuals. Perhaps it was Da Gama's exaggerated maleness that revolted him.

"He's quite a man, isn't he?" Sarah Kelso said.

"That depends on how you look at it, sweetie." Stratton lit a Turkish cigarette carefully, still keeping his gloves on. "Personally, I'm surprised to find he can walk on his hind legs. I thought the human race was supposed to have developed a little over the past half a million years."

He was certainly right about one thing—Da Gama was an animal; a soulless, mindless brute, savagely cruel and utterly sadistic. Once he got a man down he would stamp him into the ground with as little compunction as any normal individual would crush an ant.

There was a restless gleam in Desforge's eyes that didn't look too healthy and he poured himself another large whisky and laughed shortly. "You know what they say? The bigger they are the harder they fall."

"That kind of talk can be dangerous, Jack," I said. "Let me give you a few facts. Da Gama never starts a fight, he always leaves that to the other man. That way he keeps out of gaol. But he certainly finishes them. He crippled a sailor in Godthaab in June and half-killed a reindeer hunter in this very bar last month."

"What do you want me to do?" he demanded. "Genuflect?"

He didn't get any further. The door opened and Arnie Fassberg came in, Ilana on his arm. She was wearing a rather nice fur coat which looked suspiciously like real mink and she paused at the top of the stairs, her eyes searching the room till she found me. For a long moment she held my gaze, no expression on her face and then she slipped out of the fur coat and handed it to Arnie.

Underneath she was wearing that incredible dress of gold thread and tambour beading and it seemed to catch fire in the hazy light. The effect was all that she could have hoped and about the only thing in the room that didn't stop dead in its tracks was the juke box.

She finally moved, coming down the steps and crossing towards us and voices rose excitedly on every side mingling with laughter—the wrong kind of laughter. I held my breath and waited for the roof to fall in on us.

CHAPTER NINE

Desforge lurched to his feet and opened his arms to her. "And behold, there was a woman of Babylon," he declaimed.

During the hour or so that we'd already spent at the Fredericsmut he'd consumed about half the bottle of whisky he'd ordered from the bar. I think it was only then that I realised he must have been drinking for most of the day because it was the first time since I'd known him that he actually seemed the worse for liquor. His speech was slurred, his gestures slightly exaggerated and the hair falling untidily over his forehead combined with the iron-grey beard and magnificent physique stamped him as the sort of man to give a wide berth to even in a place like that.

Already people were looking our way and because of Desforge as much as Ilana. For a start just about everyone knew him, which was hardly surprising after a hundred and eleven films, the majority of which had been dubbed into most world languages. Two-fisted Jack Desforge, hero of a thousand bar-room brawls who always came out on top—every man's fantasy figure and constantly having to prove himself like some old time Western gunfighter, to any drunk with inflated ideas or the sailor on a pass who came across him in a bar and fancied his chances.

He introduced Ilana to the others and Arnie brought her a chair. Their reactions were interesting. Vogel gazed at her in frank admiration, the oldest message in the world in his eyes. Stratton was also highly impressed, but in a different way, dazzled, I suspected, as much by the golden image as anything else. Sarah Kelso managed the fixed half smile that most women seem to pull out of nowhere when faced with something they know they're going to have difficulty in competing with. Her eyes did the sort of price job on the dress and accessories that wouldn't have disgraced a computer and reluctantly admitted the final total.

Desforge put an arm round her and squeezed. "Heh, Arnie," he said. "I'm thinking of taking Ilana down to Sandvig tomorrow to do a little reindeer hunting. Can you fly us in?"

"I wish I could," Arnie told him, "but I'm flying up to Søndre in the morning."

Sarah Kelso was just about to light a cigarette and she paused and looked up at him sharply. He ignored her and smiled across at me.

"Olaf Simonsen tells me you're going to have a crack at Sule after all."

"That's right."

"I certainly hope that's an accurate met report he showed you. Rather you than me." He touched Ilana on the shoulder. "Care to dance?"

She glanced briefly at me, then pushed back her chair. "I'd love to."

"That's one hell of a good idea." Desforge stood up, swaying a little and held out a hand to Sarah Kelso. "Let's you and me show them how it's done."

Although he tried to conceal it, Vogel didn't look too pleased, but she went anyway. The juke box was playing something good and loud and the tiny floor was crowded. I watched them go, then glanced across at the Portuguese. Most of them were watching Ilana, stripping her with their eyes which was only to be expected, but the really noticeable thing about them was that they didn't seem to be talking much. Da Gama leaned back against the bar, hands in pockets, a cigarette hanging from his lips. His face was a stone mask, but his eyes followed Desforge constantly.

When I was thirteen I once found myself out on the wing in a school rugby match, very much a last minute substitution because no one else was available. My one moment of glory came when I brought down the captain of the school team a yard from the touchline, frustrating a win on the part of the other side.

He was a large, beefy individual of eighteen who gave me a thrashing in the shower rooms afterwards with the threat of worse to come if I ever got in his way again. The important thing wasn't that the experience put me off team games for life, but that it gave me a hatred of violence and a loathing for men of Da Gama's stamp, which produced a violence in return that was infinitely more frightening in its implications.

And violence was here now in this room, crackling in the air like electricity, mingling with the smoke, the human sweat, the reek of spilled liquor soaking into my brain as I breathed in so that I felt light-headed and a strange, nervous spasm seemed to pass through me in a cold wave.

And when it came it was from the most unexpected quarter. Another number started on the juke box and Ralph Stratton got to his feet without a word, pushed his way through the crowd and tapped Arnie on the shoulder. Arnie didn't look too pleased and released Ilana reluctantly.

He returned to the table and I nodded towards Stratton and Ilana. "They dance well together."

"About all he's good for I should say," Arnie commented sourly.

Da Gama spoke to one of his men, a large, dirty-faced individual in a greasy leather jerkin. The man forced his way through the crowd and tapped Stratton on the shoulder. Stratton simply shook his head and kept on dancing. The Portuguese tried again and Stratton shrugged him off, impatiently this time.

In his Savile Row suit and RAF tie the rather effeminate looking Englishman would have stuck out like a sore thumb in that kind of place even if he hadn't been dancing with the most striking looking girl in the room, and plenty of people were watching. What happened next came as a shock to most of them although I can't say it surprised me particularly.

The Portuguese pulled Stratton round and grabbed him by the lapels. It was difficult to see what happened exactly, but whatever it was, the effect was devastating. I presume Stratton must have kneed him in the groin because the Portuguese cried out sharply, his voice clear above the noise of the juke box. Stratton pushed him away and his right arm swept from behind his left shoulder, the edge of his hand slashing across the neck.

As the man went down, the crowd scattered and all hell broke loose. Stratton just had time to give Ilana a violent shove out of the way and then he had his hands full. The first of the Portuguese was almost on him. Stratton stepped back, raised his knee and flicked his foot forward. He caught the Portuguese about as low as you can go and he went down like a stone.

But the other four were by then too close for any more fancy work and swarmed all over him. Arnie was already on his way as Stratton went under, but Desforge beat him to it, roaring like an angry bull.

He grabbed one man by the neck and the seat of his pants and hurled him across the dance floor to crash headlong into a table which collapsed under his weight, scattering bottles and glasses amongst the crowd. As a woman screamed, Desforge turned his attention to one of the men who was still concentrating on Stratton, and his fist rose and fell like a club at the base of the unprotected neck.

Arnie arrived with a running jump that took him on to the back of one of the others and they crashed to the floor and rolled over and over, tearing at each other's throats. That left one man who still stood over Stratton doing his best to kick his brains out, but as I watched, Stratton rolled out of the way, grabbed at the descending foot and brought him down.

Desforge moved in to help, but he never got there. Da Gama, who had stayed at the bar watching for the twenty or thirty seconds the whole affair had taken, now intervened. Moving with astonishing speed for such a big man, he burst through the crowd and took Desforge from the rear, clamping an arm across his windpipe like an iron bar.

Both Arnie and Stratton were still fully occupied and quite obviously no one else was going to intervene as Da Gama increased the pressure. Desforge's hands tore vainly at the arm that was choking the life out of him and his face turned purple.

I began to shake, my head swelling like a balloon and the roar of the crowd was as the sea pounding in on some distant shore. I was aware of Ilana screaming at me soundlessly, then turning and hurling herself at Da Gama like a wildcat. He flung her away with his right hand and increased his grip and suddenly the stone mask dissolved into one of the cruellest smiles I've ever seen.

I suppose I must have been trying to destroy every sadistic, mindless lout I'd known in my life when I lifted the chair and smashed it across his head and shoulders. For a moment he became many people. The captain of the school rugby team who'd thrashed me as a boy, the senior cadet who'd supervised the indoctrination of recruits when I first joined the navy, and a certain commander in the Fleet Air Arm who'd pushed several young and inexperienced pilots not only to the limits of endurance, but over the edge. But most of all, he reminded me of one of the male nurses in the home where I'd undergone the cure, a walking animal who'd taken a sadistic pleasure in beating the mentally deficient into insensibility when their hysterical outbursts interfered with his card games on night duty.

The chair splintered on impact. I raised it high and brought it down again and it crumpled as the supports cracked. Da Gama cried out in pain and dropped Desforge to the floor. As he swung round, blood trickling down his face from a scalp wound, I threw what was left of the chair in his face and backed away.

He came in with a rush, hands reaching out to destroy and I dodged to one side and kicked a chair into his path so that he stumbled and fell heavily to the floor. There was a bottle of schnapps on the table at my side and I grabbed it by the neck, smashed it across the edge of the bar and had a knee on his chest before he could move.

The bottle made a fearsome weapon and I shoved the broken end up under his chin, the jagged, splintered edge drawing blood from the taut flesh. One push and he was finished and he knew it and fear broke through like scum to the surface of a pool.

109

Whether I would have killed him or not is something I'll never be sure of because a shot echoed through the roaring of the crowd, shocking me back to reality. The silence was like the calm at sea after a storm as Olaf Simonsen moved forward, an automatic pistol in his right hand.

"That's enough, Joe," he said in English. "I'll take over now."

I got to my feet and laid the bottle down very carefully on the bar. I still felt dazed and somehow outside of myself. I was aware of Da Gama lying there, of Desforge being helped to his feet by Arnie and Sarah Kelso. Stratton was still in one piece and stood at the edge of the dance floor calmly wiping blood from his cheek with a handkerchief.

Simonsen lined Da Gama and those of his men who could still stand up against the bar. Two others still sprawled unconscious on the floor and the one Desforge had thrown through the air like a sack of coals sat in a chair clutching what appeared to be a broken arm.

Simonsen came towards me, still holding his automatic and beyond him I was aware of Da Gama glaring at me as he wiped blood from his beard.

"Go home, Joe," Simonsen said in English. "And take your friends with you. I'll have a word with you all later."

I stood glaring at him stupidly and then Ilana appeared, her fur coat draped over her shoulders. She looked white and shaken, but her voice was very calm. "I think we'd better get out of here, Joe, while we still have the choice."

She held out her hand and I held on tight and followed her as meekly as a lamb.

*

Afterwards, nothing made very much sense until I stepped into the shower and shocked myself back to reality under an ice-cold spray. I gave it two full minutes which was all I could stand, then got out and towelled myself dry. As I was dressing there was a knock at the door and Arnie came in. There was a nasty bruise on his right cheek where a fist had grazed him and I noticed that his knuckles were skinned, but he was grinning cheerfully.

"Quite a night, eh? How do you feel?"

"I'll survive. How's Desforge?"

"Ilana's with him now and I'm going home to change. I've got blood all over my shirt; not mine, I'm happy to say. I'll be back in half an hour. I'll meet you in the bar."

After he'd gone, I finished dressing and went along the corridor to Desforge's room. I knocked on the door and it was opened by Ilana.

"How is he?" I asked.

"See for yourself."

He was lying on his back covered by an eiderdown, snoring rhythmically, his mouth slightly open. "The whisky finally got to him," she said. "When he wakes up he'll probably think it was all part of some crazy dream."

"I feel like that right now," I told her.

She looked up at me, her eyes serious and was obviously about to speak when there was a knock at the door. When she opened it Sarah Kelso was standing there.

"I was wondering how Mr. Desforge is?"

Ilana waved towards the bed. "If the fans could only see him now."

Sarah Kelso moved across to the bed and looked down at him. "Is he often like this?"

111

"Only four or five times a week."

Sarah Kelso placed a crocodile-leather wallet on the bedside locker. "I'll leave this here. I picked it up at the Fredericsmut. He must have dropped it during the fight."

"Are you sure it's Jack's?"

She nodded. "I looked inside. Amongst other things there was a letter addressed to him." She moved to the door and paused. "That was quite a show you put on back there, Mr. Martin. You're a man of surprises. I wonder what you'd have done if the sergeant hadn't arrived when he did."

"We'll never know now, will we, Mrs. Kelso?"

"I suppose not."

The door closed softly behind her and Ilana said, "We might as well leave him in peace. Shall we go to my room? I'd like to talk."

She lived right next door which was only to be expected, and yet I was aware of that same irrational anger I'd noticed on other occasions. It was as irritating as it was inexplicable. She was a highly desirable piece of female flesh, but she was also Jack Desforge's woman even if I did find the idea vaguely unpleasant.

She sat on the window seat and when she crossed her legs the hem of that ridiculous dress rose half-way up her thighs. She asked me for a cigarette and when I struck the match for her, my hands were shaking.

"What's Mrs. Kelso doing here exactly?" she demanded.

It was as good topic of conversation as any and I told her. She listened intently, a slight frown on her brow which was still there when I'd finished.

"Stratton seems to be very expert at taking care of himself for an insurance man," she commented. "On the other hand, you didn't do too badly back there yourself."

"I must have looked pretty crude by Stratton's standards."

"But effective," she said. "Brutally effective. Hardly the sort of thing you could have learned in the City. The trick with the bottle, for instance, wasn't exactly Queensberry Rules."

"The world I inhabited where I learnt it had only one rule. Do the other bloke before he does you."

"Will you tell me about it?" she said simply.

"Why not?" I shrugged. "It doesn't take very long. I told you I was a pilot in the Fleet Air Arm. That was back in 1951 and there was a war on of sorts."

"Korea?"

I nodded. "Don't get me wrong. It wasn't exactly the Battle of Britain. We flew coastal patrols from a carrier and the North Korean pilots weren't all that hot. But landing on an aircraft carrier's a tricky business at the best of times—they lose planes and pilots regularly even in peacetime. Most of us got into the habit of priming ourselves up in the most obvious way."

"Whisky?" she said.

"In my case, rum. But I was special—I turned out to be one of those odd birds you hear about who can't take a drink. Alcoholism is a disease, you know. Something very few people seem to realise. God knows how I survived till my time was up, but I did. The trouble was that afterwards, I found I couldn't stop."

"And that's what really broke up your marriage?"

"It certainly didn't help. I told you there was a day when I couldn't face the office any longer and simply walked out."

"And took a conversion course to make you a commercial pilot."

"I failed to mention the nine months in between. That's when I learned about broken bottles and the right place to sink a boot into a man and how to keep yourself warm and cosy on an Embankment bench with the *Evening Standard* stuffed down your shirt. I must have sampled every doss house in London by the time I was through."

"What happened?"

"I wound up in a police cell after a punch-up in some dive or another and they got in touch with Amy. She'd been looking for me for months. I might also add that she'd had to do it twice before. She got me into a home or a clinic—call it what you like—where they were doing experimental work on alcoholics. For some strange reason she seemed to think she owed me something. The rest, as they say in the books, you know."

She nodded. "But you survived, didn't you? That's the only really important thing."

"Sometimes I have my doubts."

I was standing very close to her, staring out of the window, and I looked down at those silken legs and the deep valley between her breasts that was visible through the loose neck of her dress and somehow, my hand was on her shoulder. She was in my arms instantly and I kissed her hard and long so that when she finally broke away she was breathless.

"I was beginning to think I must be slipping."

It was the sort of remark that was completely in character, I should have realised that, and yet it annoyed men and for some perverse reason of my own I wanted to hurt her.

"Are you sure Jack won't be demanding a command performance later on or don't you think he'll be up to it tonight."

She took a very deliberate step back, but there was no sudden explosion, no slap in the face—nothing so dramatic. She simply shook her head and said calmly, "You really can be very stupid for such a bright boy. Wait here, I want to show you something."

She was back in a couple of minutes holding the crocodile-skin wallet that Sarah Kelso had found at the Fredericsmut. She opened it and took out an envelope which she passed across.

"I'd like you to read that."

It was the letter Desforge had been waiting for—the one from Milt Gold of Horizon. The contents were something of a bombshell. Not only was Gold not ready to proceed with the picture—he'd had to shelve the idea permanently because the backers simply wouldn't take Jack at any price. He was sorry, but the whole thing was out of his hands. He also threw in for good measure, the news that all Desforge's California property had been seized by the court order pending the hearing of an action brought by his creditors.

I stood frowning down at the letter and Ilana plucked it from my fingers, folded it neatly and replaced it in its envelope.

"But why did he lie to me?" I said.

She shrugged. "The Mr. Micawber syndrome, lover —the desperate hope that something might turn up."

"And you knew about this?"

"That's right."

"But if there was nothing in it for you, why did you come?"

"Because I chose to—because he needed a friend, something you wouldn't understand." She stood there, one hand on her hip, very small, very defiant. "I just wanted to make it clear that I don't give command performances for anybody. Sure, I've slept with Jack Desforge on occasion, but because I felt like it and for no other reason. Now kindly get to hell out of here."

I didn't argue because something told me that we were at the stage where an attempt at an apology would be about the worst thing I could do, so I did as I was told and left.

*

When I went into the bar Arnie was sitting on a stool beside Olaf Simonsen. He got to his feet as I approached. "I was just leaving. Where's Ilana?"

"In her room, but I'd take it easy if I were you. She's in a mood to crack heads."

"Live dangerously, that's my motto," he said and went out.

I asked for a tomato juice and took the stool next to Simonsen. "When do you put the cuffs on me, officer?"

He took it half-seriously. "I don't think there'll be any need for that. How is Mr. Desforge?"

"Sleeping it off. I'll be surprised if he remembers much in the morning. What about the Portuguese?"

"They kept one of them in hospital for the night with a broken arm. Da Gama and the others are back on board their schooner with orders to stay there until it sails again which unfortunately isn't till the day after tomorrow. Still, he's finished on this coast from now on, I'll see to that." He drank some of his lager and added dryly, "On the other hand, I'm glad I arrived when I did. A killing is a killing, whoever the victim might be."

"I know," I said. "And I'm grateful."

He patted me on the shoulder and stood up. "What you need is a good night's sleep. I'll see you at the slipway in the morning."

After he'd gone I sat there thinking about a lot of

things, but Ilana kept breaking through to the surface and after a while I got up and went back upstairs. It was quiet in the corridor outside my room and I paused at the door, wondering rather bitterly how Arnie was doing. And then I heard her voice raised, sharp and clear and very angry.

I went down the corridor fast and flung open the door of her room. She was half across the bed, Arnie sprawled on top of her, laughing as he pinned her arms. I took him by the collar and yanked him away so hard that he staggered across the room against the wall, almost losing his balance. Ilana sat up, smoothing her skirt and I smiled gently.

"Anything more I can do?"

"Yes, you can bloody well get out of here and take junior with you."

There were tears in her eyes, humiliation at the thought that it had to be me of all people as much as anything else, I suspected, but as far as I was concerned she'd had enough and I turned to Arnie.

"Let's go, Arnie."

He glared from Ilana to me furiously. "So that's the way, is it? I move on and good old Joe here takes over."

The way he put it made me sound like some sort of faithful hound and I burst out laughing. "Don't be a clod. Come on, let's get out of here."

I'd never seen him so angry. "You've just made the biggest mistake of your life," he snarled at Ilana. "Here, I'll leave you something to remember me by. Stick that in your stockingtop and remember Arnie Fassberg."

He tossed something on to the bed and went out, slamming the door behind him. Whatever it was, it rolled on to the floor and Ilana got down on her hands and knees and looked under the bed. As she stood up,

I thought it was just some sort of rough pebble she was holding and then the light caught it and for a moment it glowed with green fire. Her eyes widened and I reached out quickly.

"Here, give it to me."

I held it up to the light, my throat going dry and Ilana said, "Is it worth anything?"

I dropped it into the palm of her hand. "A thousand, maybe two. It would take an expert to be sure." The expression on her face was something to be seen. "It's an emerald," I said gently. "That's what they look like before the jewellers get to work on them."

She looked completely bewildered. "I didn't know there were any emeralds in Greenland."

"Neither did I, Ilana," I said thoughtfully. "Neither did I."

CHAPTER TEN

It was almost six-thirty as I walked across to the airstrip on the following morning to get a met report. Not that I needed one—it was going to be a fine day, I could tell. Something to do with the way the ragged tracers of mist lifted off the calm water and the bold clear lines of the mountains against the sky—the sort of feeling, in fact, which can only be the product of experience. But then I was something of an old Greenland hand now which certainly gave me a sense of belonging in a way that I hadn't experienced in a very long time.

On my walk back from the tower I took a short cut past the two concrete hangars the Americans had put up in the war. A jeep stood outside the one Arnie used and as I approached the small judas gate that was set in the great sliding doors opened and the chief mechanic, a Canadian called Miller, came out with Arnie. They spoke together for a moment, then Miller got into the jeep and drove away.

Arnie turned and saw me. Something was wrong, I could tell that by merely looking at him for, as with most extroverts, ill-luck, when it came, seemed to have a physical effect on him.

"What's up?" I demanded as I approached.

He didn't bother to reply, simply opened the judas gate and went inside the hangar and I followed. The

Aermacchi crouched there in the half-light, partially on its belly, partially tilted over on one wing. Both skis were splintered and the undercarriage had been badly damaged. The villain of the piece was still on the scene, an old three-ton Bedford truck kept on the airstrip for general purpose which had obviously been backed into the Aermacchi.

"What happened?" I said.

"I haven't the slightest idea. Found her like this when I came in this morning. You know they don't have anyone down here at night. Miller thinks some drunks have probably been fooling around. Got into the truck for a lark and ended up doing this."

"Pigs could also fly," I said.

There was a long pregnant silence in which we simply stared at each other and then a moment when I suddenly felt that he was going to tell me all about it—whatever it was—but it passed.

"Miller's arranged to have the big hoist brought in. We'll soon have her up."

"What about repairs?"

"He thinks they should be able to manage here. A couple of days, that's all."

"A hell of a lot can happen in two days, Arnie," I said.

He laughed happily. "I wish I knew what you were talking about, Joe."

"So do I," I said. "Anyway, I'll have to be off." I paused as I opened the judas gate and turned. "If you find any more pebbles on the beach like the one you gave Ilana last night, save them for me will you? It's time I started thinking about my old age."

But that sort of sword-play wasn't going to get me anywhere and I left him there in the half-light, a smile on his face and fear in his eyes, and went back to the harbour.

*

Simonsen and Vogel and his party were at the slipway when I arrived and Stratton and the big policeman were already loading the skis and other items of equipment.

"What's the weather look like?" Simonsen demanded.

"Clear for most of the day. Could be some mist tonight, but if we push hard we should be in and out before it starts."

He nodded. "Let's get moving then. I've been in touch with the factor at Sandvig. He'll have a light sledge waiting for us when we touch down."

There was the sudden roar of an engine on the road behind us and the hotel Landrover approached at speed, braking to a halt a few yards away. Ilana was the first out looking like a St. Moritz tourist in her sheepskin coat, ski pants and sunglasses. The hotel porter slid from behind the wheel and started to unload the baggage as Desforge came round from the other side looking remarkably fit considering the events of the previous night.

"Top of the morning," he said cheerfully. "Almost didn't make it."

Simonsen turned to me, his eyebrows raised. "Mr. Desforge is coming with us?"

"Only as far as Sandvig," I explained. "He and Miss Eytan are going to spend a few days down there looking for reindeer."

Simonsen seemed dubious. "Something of a tight squeeze I should have thought."

He had spoken in Danish, but Desforge seemed to

get the picture and said quickly, "Look, if I'm putting you out at all, let's forget about it. Maybe I can persuade Arnie to take us after all."

"You'd have a job," I said. "He's had a slight accident with the Aermacchi. I'd be surprised to see it flying in less than three days and that's looking on the bright side."

Simonsen asked me what had happened and I explained briefly. Vogel and Stratton seemed only mildly interested, but Sarah Kelso took in every word, a bright spot of colour glowing in each cheek although the dark eyes gave nothing away. Certainly there seemed no suspicion in Simonsen's mind that the whole thing was anything more than what Miller had suggested and he nodded gravely.

"Poor Arnie—at the height of the season, too." He turned to Desforge. "If Joe thinks he can take all of us then I have certainly no objections, Mr. Desforge, but we must leave at once. We have a heavy day in front of us and I don't want to spend a night up there on the icecap if it can be avoided."

"That suits me fine," Desforge said and he paid off the driver of the Landrover and Stratton and Simonsen started to put his baggage on board.

For the briefest of moments I had a chance to speak to Ilana and moved in close, offering her a cigarette. She took it, bent her head to the match that flared in my cupped hands.

"About last night," I said quietly. "I'd be obliged if you'd keep quiet about Arnie's little present for the time being."

She seemed to gaze through me, curiously remote behind the dark glasses. "All right—but next time I see you I'll expect some light on the situation."

It was a statement of fact requiring no answer and I

didn't attempt to give one. In any case I'd other things to think about. I climbed into the cabin to check on the baggage, but Stratton obviously knew his business for it had been stacked in the best possible position relative to the pasenger load.

I packed them in one-by-one, gave the floats a last careful check, then got in myself, ran her down into the water and took off without any further delay.

*

Sandvig was fifty miles inland from the sea and protected by a maze of minor islands and fjords that cut deeply into the rocky coast. It was typical of many of the small fishing villages found in the south-west, constructed on the site of one of the old Norse settlements on a narrow shelf at the foot of the mountains, a position which gave it an unrivalled view across the sound. We touched down exactly forty minutes after leaving Frederiksborg and I took the Otter up on to a small beach.

It wasn't much of a place—there were the usual dozen or so painted houses, a small Moravian chapel and a store owned by the Trading Company which bought all the sealskins and shark liver brought in and sold in return everything the inhabitants needed.

Most of the population had already crowded down on to the narrow beach to watch with interest as Desforge and Ilana landed and we passed down the baggage. They were mostly pure Eskimo from the look of them although they all preferred to be called Greenlanders—short, sturdy figures with Mongolian features, brown cheeks touched with crimson and it was interesting to note that although some of them were in store-bought clothes, they all wore sealskin boots.

The factor from the store appeared, two men behind

him carrying the light sledge Simonsen had asked for. He spoke no English so I explained briefly about Desforge and Ilana while the sledge was being loaded.

"Everything okay?" Desforge asked.

I nodded. "I've asked him to run you up to Olaf Rasmussen's place in his jeep."

"I hope the old guy speaks some English."

"Better than you do. He'll see you all right."

"What about the return trip?"

I shrugged. "You can always get in touch with the airstrip at Frederiksborg on the radio. I'll come in for you whenever you want, always assuming I'm available."

I looked beyond him to Ilana. I wanted to say goodbye and a little more than that, but I couldn't think of the right way to put it. I believe she knew because she smiled and nodded slightly and I felt unaccountably cheerful as I climbed back into the cabin and started the engine.

It could be pretty tricky taking off from Sandvig when the wind was in the wrong direction because the far side of the fjord consisted of a thousand feet of rock wall that fell straight into green water. That morning we were lucky, lifting as effortlessly as a bird into the sky, banking across the meadows above the village as I set course and flew on between the great stone walls of the fjord towards the glacier.

*

It poured over the edge of the icecap, white lava spilling outwards like a great fan as it fell into the waters of the fjord. On either side the slopes of the mountains were carpeted by alder scrub that was nowhere more than three feet in height, but about as impenetrable as an undergrowth of rusting barbed wire. Higher up there was a clearly defined edge where the stuff stopped growing and beyond that, nothing but jagged peaks and razor-edged hogs' backs topped by snow and ice.

We slid over the crest of the glacier and drifted across a sea of ice. At this point it was under tremendous pressure. Checked by the coastal mountains, it lifted in a series of great hummocks, spilling into a thousand crevasses. It was the sort of country that was so difficult that on foot a good day's march might get you six or seven miles. I thought about the Oxford expedition and others before it, inching their way across that barren wilderness and offered up a prayer of thanks to the Wright brothers.

*

We reached Sule in forty minutes. There wasn't a trace of mist anywhere and I went in low and skimmed across the surface of the blue water. There was plenty of ice about, but mostly thin surface sheets like broken glass.

"What do you think?" Simonsen asked as I took the Otter up.

"Looks fine to me, but let's see if we can find that plane before we land. It could save us some time."

The ten miles took no more than three or four minutes of flying time, but there was no immediate sign of the Heron. I throttled back, the noise of the engine dying away to a murmur and spoke to them all over my shoulder.

"The plane should be around here somewhere so keep your eyes open. According to Arnie Fassberg it's lying in the bottom of a gully."

I banked in a wide circle and went down low and Stratton saw it almost at once, crying out excitedly, "Over there! To the left! To the left!"

I banked steeply and went down again and this time we all saw it lying there at the bottom of a deep gully just as Arnie had described, the silver and blue of the fuselage vivid against the white carpet.

I took the Otter up again and turned back to Sule, my throat dry, a coldness in the pit of my stomach that was compounded half of fear, half of excitement.

Vogel leaned forward. "How long to get there?"

"That depends on you," I said. "Or on how good you are on skis. With luck, two or three hours."

"So barring accidents we should have ample time to get there and back and return to Frederiksborg tonight?"

"If the weather holds," I said, circled the lake and landed.

It was really something of an anti-climax. The actual touchdown was no trouble at all and the only ice with which we came into contact was the thin crust that lined the shore. It cracked and splintered like treacle toffee as I ran the Otter in to the beach and cut the engine.

The silence was utter and complete and they all felt it. I turned and smiled bravely. "Let's hope the next leg goes as smoothly. All out."

I opened the door and dropped to the beach.

CHAPTER ELEVEN

The lake was surrounded by an area of bog and morass, but beyond it the dune-like plain of hummock ice stretched into infinity, the horizon shimmering in the intense white light.

I led the way as navigator, a compass dangling from my neck on a long cord and Simonsen and Vogel followed pulling the sledge by two lines secured to their waists by body harness.

I kept well out in front and paused after half an hour to take another fix and looked back at them. Vogel was obviously as expert as he had suggested and was going well, but Stratton was trailing a hundred yards to the rear. In their hooded parkas and protective goggles they all looked remarkably business-like, even Sarah Kelso sitting there in the sledge, a blanket wrapped about her legs.

I started forward again, zig-zagging between the hummocks of ice, sweating profusely at the unaccustomed exercise. It was hard work, but I was enjoying it. There was no wind and the sun was warm so that the top surface was slightly damp, sparkling in a thousand places, and I paused on top of a ridge to take my bearings again and gazed across this harsh barren landscape with a conscious pleasure.

I had told Ilana Eytan that I had come to Greenland

to make money and like most things in life that was only partly true. Perhaps Desforge romanticised too much, but when I looked out across the icecap I knew what he meant when he spoke of the alien land. Here was one of the last places on earth where the challenge was the greatest one of all—survival. Amundsen and Peary and Gino Watkins—they had all felt it, had gone forward eagerly to meet it and in some strange way I felt myself part of the same stream as I went down the other side of the ridge and made my way across the snowfield at the bottom with renewed energy.

It was criss-crossed by a hundred narrow crevasses and halfway to the other side I turned and went back to meet the others.

"Trouble?" Simonsen asked.

"I don't think so if we take it carefully. A few crevasses, that's all, but you'll need me pushing at the back of the sledge to get across."

"Perhaps I should get out and walk?" Sarah Kelso suggested.

I shook my head. "It isn't necessary, I assure you."

Stratton appeared at the top of the ridge. He paused, then glided down to join us, losing his balance and rolling in the soft slush. When I helped him to his feet he looked tired and there was sweat on his face.

"Are you all right?" I said.

He smiled brightly. "A little out of practice, that's all. I'll manage."

"It's best if we all stick together over the next stretch," I said. "It could be tricky. You can help me at the rear of the sledge."

It took us the best part of an hour to get across, heaving the sledge bodily over crevasses three to four feet wide and any depth you care to speculate. Sarah had to get off the sledge each time we came to another crevasse which didn't make things any easier. Most of them were fairly sound, but now and then a fringe of soft snow gave an illusion of safety that only Simonsen's instinct and experience saved us from.

On the other side, we took a ten-minute break and then started again, crossing easier ground this time, a rough, sprawling plain, and I made good time, stopping every ten minutes to check my position.

It was just coming up to noon when I paused on top of a rise and looked down to the plain below. What had seemed like a narrow gully from the air was in fact a sizeable ravine and without waiting for the others, I swept down the slope and did a quick stem Christie that brought me to a halt on the rim. There was nothing to be seen and I started forward, following the twisting course.

I turned a bend and the Heron lay below me, crumpled into the snow, one wing two hundred yards further on. The grave was at one side, a cairn of rocks surmounted by a rough cross fashioned from two pieces of the fuselage.

It was quiet and very peaceful and I stood there gazing down at the wreck, so wrapped up in my own thoughts that I failed to hear the approach of the others.

"Strange how it seems to fit into the landscape," Vogel said quietly.

I turned and found him at my shoulder. Simonsen was helping Sarah Kelso from the sledge and Stratton was about a hundred yards in the rear. Simonsen joined us and stood looking down at the Heron, his face serious. After a moment of silence he sighed.

"And now comes the unpleasant bit. Shall we go down?"

*

We pitched a small tent about fifty yards away from the wreck and left Sarah Kelso there with a primus stove to brew some tea, more to keep her out of the way than anything else. The next bit was going to be pretty unpleasant and there was no reason for her to be involved any more than was strictly necessary.

No digging was necessary, but the stones of the cairn had frozen together and we had to prise them apart with the two steel ice spades we had brought. Simonsen and I handled that part, but Stratton and Vogel helped by pulling each stone out of the way as it came free. I found a leg first, or what was left of one. There was still a shoe on the foot, but the shin bone gleamed through the tattered remnants of a trouser leg. Until that moment there had been a certain amount of conversation, but from then on only the chink of the spades on the cold stone disturbed the silence.

When the last stone was removed the two bodies in their shallow pit looked more pathetic than anything else. For one thing, the emotional highlights were missing. The Gothic horror of the open grave, the shrouded form in the coffin. What was left here was nothing but the framework of what had once been two human beings covered by a few tattered shreds of clothing and here and there, a strip of frozen flesh still clinging to a bone.

We stood there looking down at them for a while and then Simonsen turned to Vogel. "That photo of yours isn't going to help much here. You said Mrs. Kelso had furnished you with certain other proofs."

Vogel unzipped his parka, fumbled inside and produced an envelope which he handed to Simonsen. "Mr. Kelso's dental record."

Simonsen took out the white card contained in the envelope and got down into the pit. He tried the right-hand body first then turned his attention to the other. He got to his feet and nodded grimly.

"I'm satisfied. This one is Kelso. See for yourself."

He handed the card to Vogel who got down on his knees and made the necessary examination. When he stood up, his face was grey and sombre and he passed the card to me.

"If you would be so kind, Mr. Martin. The evidence of two completely neutral witnesses should be enough for any court."

I got down on one knee and peered into the mouth. It didn't take more than a minute to see that its contents matched the card completely. Not only was the number of teeth correct, but three gold fillings and two porcelain crowns were in exactly the right place.

I stood up and passed the card back to Vogel. "As far as I can see an identical match."

"That settles it then," Simonsen said.

"There should also be a gold signet ring on the second finger of the left hand," Vogel said. "Inside there is an inscription. *From Sarah with love*–22.2.52."

The ring was there all right, but the flesh on the finger was still intact and frozen solid. I tried to get it off without success. Simonsen dropped to one knee beside me, took out a spring-blade hunting knife and calmly sliced through the finger. He examined the ring for a moment, then passed it to me. The inscription was perfectly plain and exactly as Vogel had indicated.

There was a short silence and I said brightly, "I suppose he must just have been wearing someone else's coat."

Simonsen glanced at me sharply. "What do you mean?"

"If you look inside the jacket the name on the tab should read Harrison, isn't that right, Mr. Vogel?"

131

Vogel nodded soberly. "There was also some identification in his pocket in the name of Harvey Stein."

"He certainly liked his aliases," I said.

But Vogel was giving nothing away. "A riddle to which there can never be an answer now."

Simonsen looked interested, but obviously decided to let it go for the time being. "Better get Mrs. Kelso."

But there was no need for when we turned she was standing no more than ten yards away watching. She still wore her protective goggles so that it was. impossible to determine what was going on behind them, but her face was very white as Vogel went forward, the ring in the palm of his hand. She took off her glove and picked the ring up very delicately to examine it, and then she swayed and would have fallen if Vogel hadn't steadied her.

"Come back to the tent, my dear," he said. "There is nothing for you here."

She shook her head. "I must see him—I must!"

She pulled herself free and stumbled to the edge of the pit. I don't think she could have looked at what was left of her husband for more than ten seconds because she turned with a sharp cry and ran into Vogel's arms.

Stratton went to help and I watched them return to the tent, something very close to admiration in my heart. She was really very good. On stage at the National Theatre she could have been a household word.

*

I examined what was left of the Heron with Simonsen who made copious notes on the spot and asked my advice frequently. The wing which had parted company from the body of the plane still carried its two engines and we examined them first. They were in such a state

132

that it was impossible to say what had gone wrong. We didn't fare any better with the other two and the interior of the plane was a shambles, the instrument panel smashed into a thousand pieces.

There was still plenty of blood about, frozen into snails' trails, but when Simonsen asked me to sit in the pilot's seat I managed it with no trace of nervousness although my stomach tightened momentarily.

"Well, what do you think?" he demanded.

I shook my head. "The instruments or what's left of them, show nothing. The engines don't offer any clues. Frankly I don't think we'll ever know exactly what happened."

"Then make an intelligent guess."

"God alone knows. It couldn't have been lack of fuel because she'd been fitted with auxiliary tanks. In fact by all the rules she should have gone up like a torch when she hit the deck."

"All right, then tell me this? What were they doing up here in the first place when they should have been eight hundred miles south crossing the Atlantic?"

"Some sort of instrument error I should imagine. It's the only feasible explanation."

He nodded briskly and snapped his notebook shut. "I'll buy that. Let's go and have a cup of tea. Stratton can have his two cents' worth now."

He started back and I paused, dropping to one knee to fasten the thong on my left boot. I stayed there for rather longer than I had intended because someone had relieved himself against the side of the plane at that point. One thing was certain. It wasn't a left-over from the Oxford expedition. The yellow stain was much more recent than that. I covered it with a handful of snow and went after Simonsen.

Vogel and Stratton came to meet us. "Anything of particular interest?" the Austrian asked.

"I think the reports should be completely independent of each other," Simonsen told him. "We can compare them later."

"Certainly." Vogel nodded. "Mr. Stratton and I will get started then. The sooner we're finished, the sooner we can get out of here."

Sarah Kelso gave me tea in an aluminum cup and I drank it gratefully. She looked white and strained and seemed very subdued.

"Can I ask you how it happened?" she said.

I glanced at Simonsen who nodded. "I don't see why not."

I told her what I'd found out which wasn't a great deal anyway and volunteered as much of the guesswork as I thought might interest her.

"So it was probably just some sort of stupid error?" she said and shook her head sadly. "So much of life seems to be like that."

Simonsen leaned forward and patted her gently on the shoulder, real sympathy on his face and I got up and buckled on my skis.

"Going somewhere, Joe?" he said.

I nodded. "Just for a quick look round. I shan't be long."

I went back towards the plane, silent on my skis and paused a yard or two away. Vogel and Stratton were talking together in low tones and the Austrian's voice lifted impatiently.

"But it must be here. Try again."

I slid forward another yard and stooped so that I could see into the interior of the cabin. They crouched together just behind the pilot's seat. There was a long rent in the padded lining of the cabin and Stratton had his arm well inside.

Vogel glanced sideways and saw me and for a moment the pleasant bland mask slipped and there was murder in his eyes or something very close to it.

I waved and said cheerfully, "Have fun, I'm just going for a look round."

I moved along the ravine quickly until I found a place that gave me easy access to the top. I stood on the ridge and took a bearing with my compass. There was something I wanted to see, something I'd noticed from the air, and it couldn't be very far away.

I struck off across the plain threading my way between the hummocks, making quite good time so that I found what I was looking for within a quarter of an hour, a saucer-shaped depression about three hundred yards in diameter, a flat field of virgin snow.

But not quite. The eternal wind soon smoothed the surface up here on the icecap, but a ski plane left pretty distinctive traces. I found one or two on the far side of the depression, already partially obliterated so that only an expert would have known what they were. Much more significant was a large patch of oil and I crouched down and covered it quickly.

As I got up, someone called and as I turned, Vogel came down the slope on the far side of the depression and moved towards me quickly. I rushed to meet him, but he passed me at the half-way mark very fast with a gay cry and kept on going, doing a tremendous stem turn and sliding to a halt in a flurry of snow at the spot where I had found the oil and the ski traces. He paused, removing his goggles to clear the snow from them, glanced about him carelessly, then started towards me.

His face was bland, his eyes sparkled cheerfully, but

he'd seen everything he needed to, I couldn't have been more certain.

"I enjoyed that." He grinned. "I thought I'd better come after you. Stratton got through it all much more quickly than we'd expected."

"Did he find anything interesting?"

"Not really—did you?"

There was a nice polite smile on his face as if he really wanted to know, but two could play at that game and I smiled right back at him.

"I'm afraid not, which doesn't help you very much, does it? I suppose this affair must have cost you quite a packet one way and another."

He chuckled. "Not to worry. We always adjust to meet changing circumstances. That's the whole basis of the insurance game."

He pushed off and I watched him go, gliding effortlessly across the snow, a clever dangerous animal. I suppose I should have experienced some kind of fear as I went after him, but I didn't. Instead I was filled with a kind of strange joy and my hands shook excitedly. It was rather like one of those Saturday serials I'd seen as a kid and I couldn't wait to find out what happened in the next instalment.

*

It was almost six in the evening when we reached Lake Sule again and the strain of the day showed on everyone. The return journey had been uneventful and the weather had held, which had been my chief worry. A sudden blizzard up there on top, even the short-lived summer variety, could have proved fatal.

We loaded up quickly and as I ran the Otter down into the water a cold wind lifted off the ice, churning the surface in a sudden turbulence. Simonsen glanced over his shoulder at the horizon where grey clouds spread across the sky blotting out the sun.

"Some sort of storm on the way, Joe. We'd better get out of here fast."

I didn't need any urging. Flying half-blind through a mountain range in rough weather may be some people's version of fun, but it isn't mine. In any case, I'm just not that good a pilot. I turned into the wind, gave her full throttle and got out of there fast.

*

The real trouble came about forty minutes later when we reached the edge of the icecap and flew into the mountains. Heavy rain blew in from the sea in a grey curtain and the Otter rocked in the turbulence.

I found the head of Sandvig fjord and plunged into a cauldron of mist that reduced visibility to three or four hundred yards and was thickening by the minute.

"What do you think?" Simonsen cried above the roar of the engine.

"I think we spend the night at Sandvig," I said and went down fast while the going was good.

CHAPTER TWELVE

Olaf Rasmussen's farm occupied a commanding position on the crest of a green hill six or seven hundred feet above the village and about a mile further along the fjord. Like most of the homesteads in that part of the country, it was constructed of wood because it was warmer in winter, but in design it was quite unique. The entire length of the house at the front was made up of a hall perhaps seventy feet long and about twenty in height on the old Viking pattern with an enormous stone fireplace.

The kitchen was at the rear of the hall, half a dozen bedrooms on the first floor opening off a railed balcony. Simonsen and I shared the end one for Rasmussen had received us with his customary hospitality, informing me that Desforge and Ilana had gone up into the hills with one of the shepherds as a guide.

I was shaving in the cracked mirror above the washstand and Simonsen was lying on the bed waiting his turn for the razor when there was a step on the landing, the door was thrown open and Desforge entered.

There was a cartridge belt round his waist and with the Winchester under his arm and that wild grey beard he looked like some Corsican brigand down from the hills to rape and plunder or rather, what some Corsican brigand thought he ought to look like.

"Heh, Joe, baby, this is great!" he cried. "How did it go up there on the roof of the world. Is Mrs. Kelso still solvent?"

I nodded. "So it would appear."

"No question about it." Simonsen swung his legs to the floor and sat on the edge of the bed. "It was Kelso all right. There was a ring on his finger with an inscription as indicated by his wife before we examined him, but most important of all was his dental record. That's one thing that can't lie. In fact it's hanged more than one murderer before now."

"You don't need to tell me," Desforge said. "I've played cops on more occasions than I can remember." He turned to me. "You'll fly out in the morning I suppose?"

"If the weather clears."

He grinned. "It promises to be quite an evening. I'll see you later."

I dried my face and got dressed again, wondering what Desforge had meant. There had been a kind of affection in his eyes as if he had been genuinely pleased to see me which was perfectly possible. He was in many ways a desperately lonely man—I'd always sensed that. On the other hand, if it was an evening's drinking he was after, he'd certainly come to the right place. If any man on earth was likely to drink him under the table it was Olaf Rasmussen.

I could hear the old man bellowing at someone in the kitchen when I went out on the balcony—probably some Eskimo woman up from the village to cook for him. A door banged and he passed beneath me, a bottle in each hand and paused at the table in front of the great fireplace.

Some human beings are different from the day they are born. They have fire in their veins instead of blood and action is the juice of life to them. Olaf Rasmussen was such a man. An Icelander of Danish extraction, he had a master's ticket in both sail and steam and had lived by the sea for the first thirty years of his life, retiring to Sandvig at the age of fifty, ostensibly to raise sheep, but in reality to pursue a lifelong passion for Viking history.

Standing there in the firelight he could indeed have been one of those early settlers—Eric the Red himself, perhaps, or Leif the Lucky—an enormous patriarchal figure with hair to his shoulders and a beard that touched his chest.

As I started down the stairs he turned and, seeing me, cried out in Danish, "Lucky for me the fog came down."

We hadn't had much of a chance to talk earlier and he lit a cigar and sprawled in one of the chairs by the fire.

I said: "I don't need to ask how you've been keeping. If anything, you look younger. What's the secret?"

"Women, Joe," he told me solemnly. "I've finally given them up."

His face was very serious and I nodded gravely. "Is that so? No more Eskimo women up from the village?"

"Not more than two or three times a week. I decided it was time I cut it down."

He roared with laughter, poured himself half a glass of schnapps and swallowed it down. "And you, Joe? What about you? You look different."

"I can't think why I should."

"A woman perhaps?" I shook my head and he sighed. "Still the lonely bed. A mistake, boy. Woman was sent to comfort man. It was so ordained by the good Lord."

I decided to change the subject. "What do you think of Desforge?"

"An interesting question." He poured himself some more schnapps. "When I was twenty I was first mate on a barque out of Hamburg on the Gold Coast run. We touched at Fernando Po at the height of an outbreak of Yellow Jack." He stared into the fire, lines scoured deeply into his face at the memory of it. "There were bodies everywhere. In the waters of the harbour, in the streets. But the worst sight of all were the faces of those who knew they had it, who knew there was no hope. It was something in the eyes that told you they were already gone. Walking dead, if you like." He shook his head. "It makes me shiver to remember it even now."

"An interesting story, but what has it got to do with Desforge?"

"He has the same expression in his eyes, the same look of utter despair. Oh, not all the time. Only when he thinks you aren't watching him."

Which was quite a thought, but we were unable to take it any further because at that moment Ilana Eytan came down the stairs.

"Now this one—this one is a real woman," Rasmussen whispered, emptied his glass and went to meet her. "And how was the hunting?" he asked in English.

"Non-existent, but the scenery was magnificent. Well worth the climb." She smiled as I got to my feet. "Hello, Joe."

Rasmussen looked first at her, then at me and laughed suddenly. "So—now I understand. Good—very good. Entertain yourselves my children while I see how the dinner is coming."

"A remarkable man," she said when he had gone.

I nodded and gave her a cigarette, more for something to do than anything else. She was wearing her Norwegian sweater and ski pants and looked very small,

141

very attractive and—dare I admit it?—very desirable.

How much of this she read in my eyes I don't know, but she turned away and walked to the end of the hall, staring up at the great oaken beams, at the crossed spears and burnished shields on the wall.

"Is all this stuff real?"

I nodded. "The hall itself is only a replica of course, but it's built on the foundations of a Viking homestead a thousand years old."

"I must say Rasmussen certainly looks as if he belongs."

"He does," I said.

There was a heavy and rather awkward silence and she seemed strangely ill at ease.

"We found the plane all right," I said. "And Kelso. There was a pretty positive identification."

"Yes, Mrs. Kelso told me that much. We're sharing a room. Did anything else happen?"

"Vogel and Stratton looked very disappointed and I found a spot not too far away where someone had landed in a ski plane recently."

She was immediately interested. "Arnie?"

"I don't know anyone else on the coast who runs one."

"So the emerald Arnie gave me came from the wreck, is that what you are saying?"

"Something like that. Along with others of course."

"But how would he know they were there."

I'd been giving that question some thought on my own account and had decided there was only one plausible answer. "Sarah Kelso. She paid him a visit the first night she was in Frederiksborg. I wondered what she was up to at the time."

"Without Vogel's knowledge?"

"That's about the size of it. It certainly raises some intriguing possibilities, doesn't it?"

"What do you intend to do about it?"

I shrugged. "Why should I do anything? It's all beginning to get far too complicated for a simple soul like me."

She chuckled. "Oh, what a liar you are. What a terrible liar. I'm really going to have to do something about you."

"In which capacity? As Ilana Eytan or Myra Grossman?" I said and regretted it instantly.

The smile faded and there was something very close to pain on her face. "You won't let it alone, will you?"

I stood there staring at her, filled with self-loathing, trying to find the right words, but I was too late. Behind us Vogel and Stratton came down the stairs with Sarah Kelso and Rasmussen returned from the kitchen a moment later and I started to drown in the sudden outburst of conversation.

The meal which followed was simple but satisfying. Lentil soup, then steamed cod and a side of mutton. Afterwards there was coffee and brandy and we sat round the fire and talked, mainly about Greenland and the early settlers.

Rasmussen stood with his back to the fire, a glass in his hand and told them the beautiful and tragic story. Of the discovery of the great islands in the tenth ctntury by Eric the Red, of the thousands of Icelanders and Scandinavians who had settled the land until gradually a climatic deterioration set in making life progressively more difficult until 1410 when the last official boat sailed for home.

"But what happened then?" Sarah Kelso demanded. "What happened to those who stayed?"

143

Rasmussen shrugged. "No one really knows. The next three hundred years or so are a blank. When the missionaries came here in the eighteenth century they found only the Eskimo."

"But that's incredible."

"True, nevertheless."

There was a slight silence and Stratton said, "Do you think the Norsemen really discovered America or is the whole thing simply tales for children?"

He couldn't have chosen a better subject and Rasmussen plunged straight in. "There can be no doubt whatever that the accounts of the Norse voyages contained in the sagas are substantially true. Men sailed from here, from this very fjord. Leif the Lucky, Eric the Red's son was the first." The names rolled from his tongue, echoing from the rafters of the great hall and no one spoke. "He discovered Vinland—Vinland the Good. Probably the area around Cape Cod in Massachusetts."

"But only probably," Vogel said. "Isn't it true that most discoveries of so-called Norse relics in America and Canada have been discredited?"

"Which does not mean that there is no substance in any of them," Rasmussen said. "We read in the sagas that Leif's brother, Thorvald Eiriksson was killed in a battle with Indians, hit in the armpit by an arrow. The Danish archaeologist, Aage Roussell, excavated the farm at Sandnes up the coast from here which belonged to Thorvald's brother. Amongst other things he discovered an Indian arrowhead, undoubtedly American and a lump of anthracite coal of the same type that exists in Rhode Island. There is no anthracite in Greenland."

"Joe was telling me you do a great deal of research

144

into this sort of thing yourself," Desforge said. "Ever come up with anything?"

"A great many things. The sagas tell us that Thorfinn Karlsefne and his wife, Gudrid the Fair, settled for a while in America at a place called Straumsey—undoubtedly the Island of Manhattan. A son was born there—Snorre—the first white man born in America."

"And you believe that?" Vogel said.

"But of course. In later years he settled here at Sandvig. This very hall is built on the ruins of his homestead. I've been excavating for years."

There was real enthusiasm in his voice and they were all infected by it. "Have you anything we can see?" Vogel asked.

"Certainly." Rasmussen put down his glass, got up and led the way down to the other end of the hall and they all followed him.

It wasn't that I had no interest, but I'd seen the lovingly preserved objects that he kept on display, many times and in any case, I felt like some air. I faded into the shadows, opened the door gently and went out into the yard.

It was about eleven o'clock and at that time of the year it didn't get really dark until somewhere after midnight so that there was a sort of harsh luminosity to the rain and the mist that reminded me strongly of a Yorkshire moor at dawn.

The rain was falling very heavily now, bouncing from the cobbles, and I ran for the shelter of the barn on the far side of the yard. It was a vast, echoing place filled with the pleasant smell of new hay and a ladder led to a loft above.

It was half-full of hay and at the far end a door swung to-and-fro in the wind, a fine spray of rain drifting in. There was a clear drop of thirty feet or so to the cobbles below and a heavy hook and pulley swung from a wooden hoist. Altogether it was a sort of paradise one had loved to play in as a boy and I resisted a strong impulse to slide down the rope to the ground, and lit a cigarette and stood looking out at the rain, filled with a pleasant nostalgia.

The main door creaked below and Ilana called softly, "Joe?"

I crouched at the edge of the loft and looked down at her. She was dressed as she had been for dinner with the addition of the sheepskin coat which was draped over her shoulders.

She glanced up, saw me and smiled. "Is there room for one more up there?"

"I think so."

She climbed the ladder and stood looking about her, hands in pockets. "This is nice. Why did you cut out? Weren't you interested?"

"Fascinated," I said. "Always have been, but Olaf Rasmussen and I are old friends. I've seen it all before. Anyway it was suddenly too crowded in there. Too many people I don't like."

"Does that include me?"

"What do you think?"

We moved along to the open door. She sat on a box and I gave her a cigarette.

"Do you often feel like that? Hemmed in, I mean."

"Frequently."

She smiled and shook her head. "You told me you came to Greenland because you could make more money here than anywhere else. That isn't really true, is it?"

I looked out into the rain, trying to get it straight in my own mind. "In the City I worried about where I was going to park the car. When I found somewhere, I worried about overparking. Here, each day is a new struggle—people against the wilderness. It keeps a man on his toes. One of the few places left on earth that can give you that feeling."

"For how much longer?"

I sighed. "That's the trouble. Icelandair has started running four-day tourist trips from Iceland to Narssarssuaq which isn't all that far from here. There's a good airfield and a reasonable hotel. I've a nasty feeling it's the beginning of the end. It always is once the tourists start coming in."

"And what will you do then?"

"Move on."

"With a brand new persona, I suppose?"

I frowned. "I'm not with you."

"It's a term Jung used. He argued that most people can't face life in real terms so they invent a persona for themselves—a new identity if you like. We all suffer from the same disease to a greater or lesser degree. You try to present the image of a tough bush pilot, a strong man with steel nerves who can handle anything that comes along."

"Is that a fact now?"

She carried on: "Rasmussen sees himself as a latter day Viking. Jack's trouble is that he's had to create and discard so many different identities that he's long since lost any kind of contact with reality."

"And where in the hell do you get all this stuff from?" I demanded.

"I read psychology and social philosophy for a year at university."

Which took the wind right out of my sails and I stared at her in astonishment. "Why didn't you continue?"

She shrugged. "I just felt that it wasn't for me, that those dons and lecturers with their heads in their books were living the biggest lie of all."

I shook my head. "Strange, but I thought I was getting to know you and suddenly, I find you're a complete stranger."

"What did Jack tell you about me?" she said.

"About Myra Grossman," I corrected her. "The poor little East End Jewess with a chip on her shoulder and a father with a tailor's shop in the Mile End Road."

"He must have forgotten to tell you about the other one hundred and sixty-three branches," she said gently.

I stared at her blankly. "But why should he do that?"

"Jack's a very complex character. Did he say anything else about me?" I nodded slowly. "Anything I should know?"

I shook my head. "Nothing important—nothing I believed."

"You're a poor liar, Joe." She smiled gravely. "Drinkers—real drinkers don't have much interest in sex. I should have thought you would have known that."

I nodded slowly. "I seem to have taken rather a lot for granted. I'm sorry about that. Do you believe me?"

"I could give it a try."

"Then tell me one thing? Why *did* you come out here? That's the one thing I still can't understand."

She said: "It's really very simple. I wanted to be an actress and money can't buy you that, only talent. Jack helped me along, got me into pictures. All right, I'm certainly not the greatest thing since Bernhardt, but I can get all the work I want now. They come to me."

"And you feel guilty about that? You think you owe him something?"

148

"He was badly in need of financial backing for this picture, the one that's folded. I thought I could interest my father. In fact the truth is that Jack took the whole thing as read."

"And your father wouldn't play?"

"I felt the least I could do was face him especially when Milt Gold told me the whole deal was off now." She shook her head. "Poor Jack."

"I find it difficult to cry in my beer over a man who's gone through three or four million dollars in his lifetime," I said.

"I don't. I feel personally responsible."

"That's crazy." I don't know why, but I grabbed her arm and pulled her to her feet. "You want to cut that sort of thinking right out for a start."

Suddenly, she was against my chest and we were kissing, my arms fast around her. She came up for air and smiled, her eyes wide.

"Are you quite sure this is what you want?"

"Ever since I saw you in the saloon on the *Stella* in that ridiculous gold dress."

"Let's get our terms of reference straight before we go any further," she said and pushed me away. "Do you want to make love to me or me in that kinky dress? There's a difference."

"I'll have to give that at least ten seconds thought," I said, but as I reached out for her, the door creaked in the barn below and we heard voices.

I put a finger to my lips and tiptoed to the edge of the platform. Desforge was standing with his arms around Sarah Kelso. As I watched, he picked her up in his arms and carried her across to the hay.

I moved back cautiously to Ilana. "Remember what you were saying about drink and the flesh? Well Jack's

149

down there in the hay with Sarah Kelso right this minute and it doesn't seem to be bothering him one little bit."

She held one hand hard against her mouth to contain her laughter and I took her by the arm and led her to the open door and the hoist.

"In case you're interested that's the only way out."

She shook her head. "Not for me, I never was the athletic type."

"So what do we do?" I said.

*

It was a good hour later and quite dark, when Desforge and Sarah Kelso left. I helped Ilana down the ladder and we moved through the darkness to the door. It was still raining heavily and we stood there for a moment, my arm around her waist.

"Ready?" I said.

She nodded and we ran across the yard together. We paused on the steps of the porch, laughing, and Desforge said from the shadows, "That you, Joe? I've been wondering what happened to you."

For a moment, I thought he was going to make trouble. Instead he said, "Look, I've decided I've had this place. Any chance of flying out with you in the morning?"

"That's fine by me."

"See you at breakfast then."

The door closed softly behind him and I looked down at Ilana. "What do you make of that or does he think he's in love?"

"He doesn't know what the word means."

Her face was a pale shadow in the darkness as I held her away from me and looked at her searchingly. "Do you, Ilana? Do you know what it means?"

"I like what happened back there in the loft," she said. "I like you. That's enough for one night. Step by step, Joe Martin. Step by step."

She didn't even kiss me good night. Simply left me to think about it, standing there in the darkness listening to the rush of the heavy rain, smelling the earth, and something seemed to melt inside me so that I felt like laughing out loud for the first time in years.

CHAPTER THIRTEEN

We flew out of Sandvig just after dawn and landed at Frederiksborg by eight. I got rid of my passengers and started to make up for lost time. I took a couple of miners into Godthaab and carried on to Søndre Strømfjord to pick up some machine parts needed urgently by a deep sea trawler which had come into harbour with engine trouble.

I arrived back in Frederiksborg at one o'clock to find Simonsen clamouring to be taken to a fishing village about a hundred miles up the coast where some Eskimos had been trying to stick harpoons into each other instead of the seals. I dropped him off, promising to return on the following afternoon, and flew back to Frederiksborg.

It was the first opportunity I'd had to look up Arnie and I went to the air strip. The Aermacchi was there, raised on a couple of chain hoists and Miller and two mechanics were working on the undercarriage.

"Where's Arnie?" I said.

"Haven't seen him since last night." Miller grinned and wiped his hands on an oily rag. "Probably been in bed with some dame all day. A couple of other guys were looking for him. They were back again just after noon. Didn't seem to be having much luck."

"Who were they?"

"The older one was called Vogel. Sounded like a German or something to me."

"Austrian," I said. "Not that it matters. How's the work coming along?"

"Just fine. He should be able to take her up tomorrow. Tell him that if you see him, will you?"

So the hounds were closing in? I hurried back to town and called at his house but the front door was locked and there was no reply to my knock. That left two possibilities. He was either with Gudrid or drinking at the Fredericsmut which was on my way to the hotel anyway, so I decided to call.

It had been one hell of a day. The kind that needs a couple of double brandies to add zest to it so I ordered black coffee, sat on one of the high stools at the bar and pretended I was a drinking man.

I asked the barman if Arnie had been in and he nodded. "Earlier this afternoon about one o'clock. He had something to eat here and then two men came in and joined him—the ones who were with you the other night. There was some trouble. I don't know what it was exactly, but he cleared out."

"What kind of trouble?"

He shrugged. "I was in the back, but Sigrid was here. Just a minute, I'll get her."

He went into the kitchen and a couple of minutes later, the impudent looking young Eskimo girl who'd served us on my last visit came in. She was obviously in the middle of baking and wiped flour from her hands with a towel.

Her English was about as basic as you could get, so we talked in Danish. Arnie had been half-way through his meal when the two men came in. She couldn't understand what they were saying because they talked in English, but the older man had got very angry and it seemed Arnie had laughed at him. What happened then, she wasn't sure, but there had certainly been some sort of scuffle because a chair had gone over and Arnie had left in a hurry.

I thanked her and she returned to the kitchen. I sat there drinking my coffee and thinking about the whole thing, then went to the telephone, rang the hotel and asked for Gudrid.

She sounded cautious when she came to the phone. "Who is it?"

"Joe Martin. I'm looking for Arnie."

She hesitated rather obviously. "He told me to tell no one where he was this afternoon. Said he wanted some peace and quiet."

"This is important, Gudrid—really important. Now where is he?"

"All right," she said. "He's gone fishing."

"The usual place."

"As far as I know."

"Fine—I'll catch up with him there."

I put down the receiver and checked the time. It was five-thirty and the usual place was two miles on the other side of the fjord which meant borrowing a boat, not that that would present any difficulty. I left quickly and hurried through the rain towards the harbour.

*

Fog crouched on the lower reaches of the fjord and the steady drizzle indicated a dirty night to come as I left the harbour. I'd borrowed an inflatable rubber dinghy powered by a large outboard motor that gave a surprising turn of speed.

Four icebergs moved majestically down towards the sea, strung out line-astern like battleships, ranging in colour from purest dazzling white to blue and green.

154

There was a sudden turbulence in the water to starboard as a piked whale surfaced, white flukes and belly gleaming as it rolled and went under again.

There was beauty and excitement in just being there with the prow lifting out of the water and the rain cold on my face, but none of it really registered. I had to see Arnie, had to have the whole thing out with him, I knew that now.

I found him drifting in an old whaleboat about a mile further on, fishing for cod with a hand line. He was wearing an oilskin coat and sou'wester and I noticed a double-barreled shotgun under the seat.

I tossed him a line and he pulled me close. I climbed into the whaleboat and joined him. "You're a difficult man to find. I've just seen Miller, by the way. He says you should be airborne again by tomorrow."

"That's nice to know," he said cheerfully, and passed me a Thermos. "Hot coffee—help yourself."

He returned to his fishing, dropping a spoon-shaped spinner over the side and I shook my head. "You never learn do you? There's no need for that. Even a bare hook will do. Cod are bottom feeders. All you have to do is jig it up and down—like this."

I took the line from his hand and said casually, "What have you done with the emeralds, Arnie?"

"Emeralds?" His face was as innocent as a child's. "What on earth are you talking about?"

"The emeralds you found in the wreck of that Heron up there on the icecap, the ones Sarah Kelso told you about. Before you try denying it I'd better tell you that I found tracks where a ski plane had landed and a patch of oil about half a mile from the crash."

"Am I the only person in the world with a ski plane?"

"The only one in these parts—the only one who makes presents of uncut emeralds worth forty thousand krone. That was really very rash of you, Arnie, letting your temper get the better of you like that."

His face hardened. "Why don't you try minding your own business, Joe?"

I ignored him and carried straight on. "When we bumped into Sarah Kelso outside of her room that night, I think she got the impression that she'd scored a big hit—that you were so besotted you'd do anything for her, which she saw as a golden opportunity to put one over on Vogel. You could fly in, pick up the emeralds, then return with the tale that any kind of a landing was impossible."

Most of this was simply intelligent guesswork based on the few facts I did have for certain, but from the expression on his face I was on the right track, so I carried on.

"You even tried to stop me from going in by insisting that a floatplane landing wasn't possible because there was too much ice on Lake Sule. I suppose the plan was for the two of you to fly off into the sunset together, only you weren't quite as sold on her as she'd imagined and came up with a better idea. At a guess I'd say you told her you hadn't been able to land, which, after all, had always been a possibility. She didn't trust you, especially when you let slip the fact that you were flying out the following morning—the day the rest of us were leaving for Sandvig, so she went down to the airstrip, started up that old truck and rammed the Aermacchi just to make sure you wouldn't be leaving."

He had listened without a murmur, but now he said, "There was a Catalina in from Søndre yesterday afternoon. I could have flown back there as a passenger and caught a jet to Canada or Europe."

I shook my head. "Not with the emeralds on your person—too big a risk with Customs to go through, especially if they're in the quantity they must be to make this whole thing worthwhile. No, you needed the Aermacchi in the air for the scope it gave you. Lots of possible hiding places on board and the freedom to fly anywhere you wanted. That's why you've hung on here and after all, you've very little to worry about. Sarah Kelso couldn't be certain you were double-crossing her and she couldn't very well tell Vogel. With luck you might have been away today, but now it's too late. Now they're back and after your blood. Vogel knows a ski plane landed up there and from the look of him I shouldn't imagine he has much trouble with simple addition."

He didn't attempt to deny any of it now. "I can look after myself," he said sullenly.

I felt the sort of annoyance you experience with a stubborn child who refuses to see sense. "For God's sake, Arnie, these men are pros. They've been carving up suckers like you all their lives."

I suppose it was a mixture of fear and resentment that made him erupt so violently or perhaps it was quite simply that he'd never really liked me.

"Who in the hell do you think you are? Half a man who vomits at the first whiff of a barmaid's apron. Do you think I need you to tell me what to do? Help me, you say? You can't even help yourself." He pulled the shotgun from under the seat and held it up. "Let them come, that's all I ask. Just let them come."

It was grotesque, it was ludicrous and there was nothing I could do, nothing I could say. I suppose I could have turned him in. I could have gone straight to Simonsen, but then he couldn't have done very much, not without some convincing proof and I hadn't any. In any case, I just didn't want to be involved—it could lead to too many complications. I might even have to do some explaining myself and that was the last thing I wanted.

There was a tug as the hook was taken and I hauled in a cod which looked all of three pounds. Instinctively, Arnie clubbed it with the butt of the shotgun.

"At least I've managed to take care of your supper for you," I said. "I wouldn't stay out much longer if I were you. This fog is going to get worse before it gets better."

He didn't reply; just sat there, his face very white under the black sou'wester, clutching the shotgun to his chest, fear in his eyes—real fear. And I left him there, which on looking back on it was the worst thing of all. Instead of trying again, I climbed into the dinghy, pressed the starter button on the outboard and moved away rapidly through the gathering fog.

*

By the time I had reached the harbour the fog had wrapped itself around me in a damp grey shroud, but I made the anchorage safely, tied up the dinghy and mounted the steps to the jetty.

Somewhere a foghorn sounded as a trawler moved in cautiously, but otherwise it was completely silent as I went along the jetty. I'd left the Otter at the top of the slipway, but I hadn't refuelled her so I set to work, bringing two jerrycans at a time from the stockpile, emptying them and returning for more. It took me all of twenty minutes and by the time I'd finished I was damp with sweat. At one point I heard footsteps approaching and a seaman loomed out of the fog and disappeared again along the jetty without speaking. I might have been the last person alive in a dead world.

I emptied the last can and started to secure the Otter for the night, lashing her down to the ring bolts. At one

point I turned suddenly, staring into the fog behind me.
I hadn't heard anything and yet I had the feeling that I
was being watched, that somewhere just out of sight a
presence was waiting for me.

Stupid and illogical perhaps, and yet my flesh crawled
and I turned quickly to finish my task. I heard nothing
and yet there was the feeling of movement behind me
like a turbulence in the air. I started to rise, but I was
too late. Someone delivered a stunning blow to the base
of my neck and I went down hard. For a moment I lay
there, my face against the wet concrete. Something
enveloped me, wet and clinging, stinking of fish, and
then there was only the darkness.

*

It was like coming up from deep water, drifting
through layer after layer of darkness towards the light
seen dimly like the dawn through ragged grey clouds.
I finally surfaced, my eyes wide and staring. My head
ached and for a little while I couldn't even remember
who I was or what I was doing here. Strangely enough
the link between this world and the old was the last
thing I had remembered, the stink of fish, which wasn't
surprising as I was lying on a pile of damp nets.

I was in the hold of a ship, probably a trawler from
the look of it, although the light was so bad that I could
only detect the vague outline of things. There was a
hollow drumming as someone moved along the deck
above and I sat up.

There was a mild explosion in my head as I closed
my eyes involuntarily, clenching my teeth against the
pain. Deep breathing was the thing. I tried it for a
while and felt a little better.

I got to my feet and stumbled through the gloom,
hands outstretched before me until I came to a hatch-

way above my head, light gleaming faintly through the cracks where it fitted unevenly. It was at least four feet above my head so I did the obvious thing and started to shout.

Footsteps sounded on the deck again, the hatch was pulled back and someone looked down at me. He was just a seaman with a greasy woollen cap on his head, a face like Spanish leather and the sort of long drooping moustache the gunfighters used to wear out west. I recognised him at once as one of the men who'd been with Da Gama at the Fredericsmut on the night we'd had all the trouble.

Which didn't make any kind of sense unless Da Gama was engaged in some sort of private vendetta. The man looking down at me gave no clue. In fact he replaced the hatch and went away again.

I sat down, my head in my hands, and tried some more deep breathing. It didn't work particularly well because suddenly the darkness and the pain and the stench of rotting fish all seemed to come together and I rolled over and vomited.

I felt a little better after that. According to my watch, which still seemed to be working, it was seven o'clock when the sailor went away. It was a good hour later when the hatch was removed and he reappeared.

This time Da Gama was with him. He squatted on his haunches and peered down at me, a cigar clenched between his teeth, the sort of expression on his face that a cat has with a mouse between its paws.

He turned and said something and a moment later a ladder came down. By that time I was too weak to feel anything, even fear, and I scrambled up and collapsed on the deck, sucking in great lungfuls of damp sea air.

He crouched beside me, a look of concern on his

face. "You don't look too good, Mr. Martin. How do you feel?"

"Bloody awful," I said weakly.

He nodded soberly and then took his cigar from between his teeth and quite deliberately touched the glowing end to my cheek. I yelled like a stuck pig, rolled away from him and scrambled to my feet.

The sailor took a knife from his belt and moved towards me and Da Gama laughed harshly. "Feel better now, Mr. Martin? That's good, eh? That sharpens you up a little?"

I looked around me wildly and the sailor prodded me in the back, the tip of the knife slicing through my clothes and drawing blood. Da Gama tossed off an order in Portuguese, turned and moved along the deck and the sailor pushed me after him.

We went down the schooner's stern companionway and Da Gama opened the door of the cabin at the bottom and stood to one side. He nodded to the sailor, obviously dismissing him, grabbed me by the shoulder and threw me inside so that I lost my balance and went sprawling.

I lay there for a moment, the darkness moving in on me again and then a familiar voice said, "I say, old chap, you are in a mess, aren't you?"

Ralph Stratton pulled me up from the floor and dumped me in a chair. When I managed to focus I found Vogel sitting on the other side of the table.

CHAPTER FOURTEEN

My cheek was on fire where Da Gama had burned me, but the pain in my head had eased into a kind of dull throbbing. My hands were shaking slightly, but that was reaction, I suppose, and I made a conscious effort to steady them. At least my brain was starting to function and I don't think I'd ever felt so frightened in my life before. If Desforge had been playing the part the scriptwriters would have given him something witty to say, or perhaps he'd have reached for the bottle of cognac and one of the glasses that stood on the table, helping himself with the sort of off-hand bravado with which tough heroes always faced that kind of situation.

But this was me, Joe Martin, weak as a kitten and sick to my stomach because I had a strong suspicion that whatever happened now, I was going over the side somewhere out to sea with a weight around my feet. I might come up again, or what was left of me, when the ice thawed next spring, but it was more than likely that no one would ever hear of me again.

Or perhaps I was just being melodramatic. I wiped sweat from my face with the back of one hand and said in a cracked voice, "I wish someone would tell me what this is about."

"Don't be stupid," Vogel said crisply. "You're well aware why you're here."

There was a sudden unexpected diversion on deck, a shout of anger, a flurry of blows and drunken voices arguing fiercely. Da Gama went out without a word and I said to Vogel, "Where does he fit in?"

"A blunt instrument. If the price is right and I asked him to, he would dispose of you without the slightest hesitation. You would do well to remember that."

The silence hung between us and he left it there for a while, probably for effect. "When we reached the Heron yesterday I expected to find something which belonged to me—something which had been carefully concealed. It was missing. Do you know what I'm talking about?"

I shook my head. "I haven't the slightest idea."

"Then why did you keep quiet about your discovery that a ski plane had landed recently in the area?"

I tried to think of a suitable reply to that one and failed miserably. "Did I?"

Stratton sighed. "You're really being very stupid, old chap."

I noticed that he was still wearing those black leather gloves of his which didn't make me feel any better, especially when he moved around behind me.

Vogel said: "There is only one ski plane operating on the coast at the moment, you told me that yourself."

There was no point in denying it and I didn't try. "That's right."

"Which would seem to indicate that Fassberg lied to us when he returned from his reconnaissance flight and announced that a landing was out of the question. Why would he do that?"

"Why not ask him?"

"I have done, but he wasn't in the mood for conversation. When I have your contribution to this mystery, we'll try again." He poured himself a brandy and leaned back in the chair. "I'll ask you for the second

163

time. Why did you conceal the fact that Fassberg had landed in the vicinity of the crash."

I decided to try a little improvisation. "All right, I'll tell you. He's a friend of mine. I didn't know what his game was. On the other hand I didn't want to be the one to land him in any kind of trouble so I decided to keep my mouth shut till I'd seen him."

"And have you?"

"I haven't had the chance yet. I've been flying all day."

Vogel sipped a little of his brandy, held up the glass to the light and shook his head. "No, Martin, it won't do. It won't do at all." He put down his glass very deliberately and leaned forward. "You're lying—you're holding something back. Shall I tell you how I know? Because I've looked into your eyes, because I've watched your reactions, listened to what you have said and none of it makes sense—none of it!"

His last few words were shouted into my face and Stratton struck me across the back of the skull with his knuckles so that I cried out in pain. He yanked me back by the hair and clamped an arm across my throat.

"Let's try again," Vogel said. "Fassberg landed in his ski plane, went to the Heron and removed what I came to Greenland to recover. Wouldn't you say that was a reasonable assumption?"

"Only if he knew what he was looking for," I said.

The thought must have occurred to him before, because it just couldn't be avoided and he sat there staring at me. This time you could have sliced the silence with a knife and Stratton said slowly. "I'd say he's got a point there."

"Of course he has, you fool." Vogel leaned forward. "Who, Martin? Who could have told him?"

"That's something you'll have to work out for yourself, but it would need someone who knew in the first place, wouldn't it? Someone close to you." I looked up at Stratton. "What about our friend here? How long has he been around?"

Stratton's hand rose and fell, catching me across the side of the head and I almost lost my senses. I slumped forward, head in hands, fighting the pain, and Vogel said, "Bring him round, you fool. I haven't finished with him yet."

There was the chink of the decanter, then Stratton wrenched back my head and poured half a glass of brandy into my mouth. As the nausea hit me there was the usual body-wrenching spasm and I vomited all over his neat grey suit. He gave a cry of disgust, sent me away from him with a tremendous heave and the chair went over. I rolled to the wall and got up as Stratton started to unbutton his jacket. When he had it half off, I sucked in some air, grabbed for the door handle and plunged outside.

He almost had me on the companionway, but I kicked out and caught him full in the face. And then I had the door open and was out on deck. Da Gama was standing no more than three or four feet away talking to a couple of his crew. As he swung round, I kept on going and vaulted the rail. The shock of the icy water was so terrible that for a moment I thought the heart had stopped beating inside me, but then I surfaced and struck out wildly into the fog.

*

I knew they'd expect me to get out of that freezing water at the earliest possible moment, which meant they'd be strung out along the jetty waiting for me. I took a chance and headed through the fog to the other side of the harbour.

It took me no more than ten minutes, but towards the end I didn't think I was going to make it and then my knee banged against a submerged rock. A few moments later I crawled out of the water and fell face down on a shingle beach.

I was numb with cold, but I forced myself to my feet and stumbled across the beach to a broken line of massive concrete blocks which I recognised as being part of the defensive system laid down at the northern end of the air strip against winter storms.

I checked my watch. It was almost nine, about three hours since my meeting with Arnie on the other side of the fjord. He would have returned by now, probably not long after me in view of the deterioration in the weather.

I ran across the airstrip, flapping my arms vigorously to try and get some feeling back into them. There was no one about as far as I could see and the hangars were deserted, so I borrowed an old jeep that was kept for general use about the place. Whatever happened now I had to make Arnie realise the kind of people he was dealing with and I drove towards town as fast as the fog would let me.

I parked the jeep at the end of the narrow street and walked towards the house. As I reached the steps leading up to the veranda, the side gate banged and someone ran out of the fog wildly. I had a momentary glimpse of Gudrid Rasmussen's face, eyes wide and staring, and then she was gone.

I hammered on the front door. There was no reply, but the curtain was drawn and a chink of light showed through. I tried again, calling his name with no better success and went round the side of the house and tried the kitchen door.

I think I knew what I was going to find the moment I

stepped inside. For one thing there was a special quality to the silence. It was as if the whole world had stopped breathing and the harsh distinctive odour of gunpowder hung on the air.

The living room was a shambles. The telephone had been ripped from the wall, drawers turned out, cushions torn apart, books scattered across the floor and blood —fresh blood—splashed across the wall in a crimson curtain.

Arnie lay on his back on the other side of the couch, most of his face missing, his own shotgun lying across his body where the murderer had dropped it. Strange, but at times, the face of Death can be so appalling that it freezes the soul, cutting out all emotional response, preventing any normal reaction. I stood staring down at him, trapped in a kind of limbo where nothing was real any more and all that had happened seemed part of some crazy nightmare.

Somewhere a shutter banged, blown by the wind, bringing me back to reality like a slap in the face and I turned and ran as if all the devils in hell were at my heels.

*

I parked the jeep in the courtyard at the rear of the hotel and went up the back stairs to my room. When I opened the door Ilana was sitting by the window reading a book. It seemed as if I was still back there in the fog as her face jumped out to meet me, the smile of welcome fading into a look of astonishment and concern.

I'm not quite sure what happened after that. I only know that I was on my knees and her arms were tight around me. I don't think I've ever been so glad to see anyone in my life before.

167

*

I had a hot shower and changed and told her everything. When I'd finished, we did the obvious thing and went along to Gudrid's room. The door was locked, but I knocked several times and called her name and after a while it opened and she gazed out at us fearfully. Her eyes were swollen from weeping and she was shaking as if she had a fever.

She looked at me and then at Ilana and pushed back a tendril of hair that had fallen across her eyes. "I'm sorry, Mr. Martin, I don't feel very well. I'm going to take the rest of the night off."

I shoved her back into the room and Ilana followed me. "I saw you leaving, Gudrid," I said.

She looked genuinely bewildered. "Leaving? I don't understand."

"Outside Arnie Fassberg's place. You ran straight past me. I was on my way in."

Her face crumpled and she turned and flung herself on the bed, her body racked by great sobs. I sat down and patted her on the shoulder. "There's no time for that, Gudrid. Have you told the police?"

She turned her tear-stained face to look up at me. "I didn't kill him, you must believe that. He was dead when I arrived."

"I believe you," I said. "You've nothing to worry about."

"But you don't understand. Arnie and I often quarrelled—plenty of people knew that. Sergeant Simonsen knows it."

"He also knows what's possible and what isn't and the idea that you could have let Arnie Fassberg have both barrels in the face at point-blank range is so preposterous that he wouldn't even waste his time considering it." I took her hands and held them tight. "Now tell me what happened?"

"I got a phone call from Arnie about forty minutes ago. He asked me to bring round a package I've been looking after for him. He said he knew that I was on duty, but that I must bring it. That it was a matter of life and death."

"Did you know what was in the package?"

She nodded. "He told me they were ore specimens that had come into his possession, evidence of mineral deposits somewhere in the mountains that would make him a wealthy man. He told me to keep the package in the safest place I could find. He said our whole future depended on it."

"What future?"

"We were to be married, Mr. Martin."

She started to cry again, a handkerchief to her mouth and Ilana sat down and put an arm round her. I got to my feet and walked to the window. Poor little bitch. So much in love that she'd been willing to believe anything, even a story as shot full of holes as an old skein net.

After a while she seemed to regain some kind of control and I tried again. "So you took the package round?"

She shook her head. "I didn't have it to take. I know it's silly, but I was frightened to death—afraid I might lose it or that it might be stolen—there's been a lot of petty theft in the staff quarters lately. Another thing, you know what a terrible gambler Arnie was. He was always giving me money to look after for him one day and asking for it back the next. For the first time I seemed to have him pinned down. I wanted to keep it that way so I posted the package to myself and addressed it to my grandfather's farm at Sandvig. It went with the monthly supply boat first thing this morning."

"What happened when you told Arnie that?"

"That was the strangest thing of all. He started to laugh and then the phone went dead."

I nodded to Ilana. "Whoever was with him must have ripped it out then."

"I was worried and anxious," Gudrid carried on. "So I got my coat and slipped out the back way even though I was supposed to be on duty."

"And he was dead when you got there."

She stared into space, horror on her face, and said in a whisper, "I think I heard the shots as I went down the street, but I can't be sure. The front door was locked so I went round to the back. And then I saw the blood on the wall. Oh, dear God, the blood."

She broke down completely and I left Ilana to comfort her and went to the window. After a while she joined me. "So it was all for nothing."

"All for nothing," I said. "It's difficult to think of him as dead. He was so full of life."

She put a hand on my arm. "You'll have to go to the police now, Joe."

"Not yet," I said. "There's someone else I want a word with first."

"Sarah Kelso?"

"That's right. Her reaction to this should be very interesting. I'll see if she's in her room."

"You'd be wasting your time," she said. "She's with Jack. As far as I know they've been together all evening."

"She'll just have to get out of bed then, won't she?" I said. "You'd better hang on here."

"Oh, no you don't." Ilana brushed past me and opened the door. "I wouldn't miss this for all the tea in China."

*

Desforge's door was locked and I knocked and kept on knocking until I heard sounds of movement inside. When he opened it he was still tying the cord of his dressing gown, his hair was rumpled and he didn't look pleased.

"What in the hell is this?" he demanded.

I forced my way past him and Ilana followed me. "Get her out here, Jack," I said.

He stared at me open-mouthed, then slammed the door and moved in belligerently. "Now look here, Joe . . ."

I crossed to the bedroom door, opened it and said crisply, "Mrs. Kelso, I thought you might be interested to know that someone just murdered Arnie Fassberg."

I closed the door again and moved back to the others. Ilana helped herself to a cigarette from a box on the table and Desforge stared at me, his mouth slack.

"You don't sound as if you were kidding, Joe."

"I wasn't, believe me."

He moved to the side table where several bottles and glasses stood on a tray and poured himself a drink mechanically. "And you're saying she's mixed up in this in some way."

"That's about the size of it."

The door opened behind me and when I turned, Sarah Kelso was standing there, her face very white. She was wearing a button-down jersey dress that had obviously been pulled on in some haste and her hair was all over the place.

"I believe you said something about Arnie Fassberg, Mr. Martin."

"That's right," I said. "He's dead. Somebody used

171

his own shotgun on him—both barrels in the face at point-blank range."

She swayed and Desforge hurried to her side and helped her to a chair. "You're very kind," she said weakly.

I poured some brandy into a glass and carried it across to her. "A lot kinder than Vogel and Stratton will be when they get their hands on you. You tried to double-cross them, didn't you? There were emeralds hidden in that plane in the roof of the cabin near the pilot's seat. You told Arnie. You persuaded him to drop in on that first day and recover them, then fly back here and pretend that a landing was impossible."

"He told me that he hadn't been able to land," she said, gripping her glass with both hands. "He lied to me."

"But you couldn't be sure, could you?" I said. "Not until the rest of us had reached the Heron, and by that time he might be gone, so you went down to the airstrip at night, started up that old truck and ran it into the Aermacchi."

She nodded wearily. "All right—I'll tell you. I'll tell you everything. Vogel is the kind of man who has an interest in many things. Some legal—some a little bit on the shady side."

"What about the London and Universal Insurance Company?"

"It's a legally constituted company. I know it must be because it paid me out on my husband's death just like Vogel told you."

"What about your husband? Where did he fit into all this?"

"Jack was flying for a Brazilian internal airline. Just a fill-in job till he got fixed up with one of the big companies. He met this man Marvin Gaunt in a bar in São Paulo. He said he'd bought a Heron secondhand from some rich Brazilian, but couldn't get an export licence. He offered Jack five thousand dollars to fly it out illegally to a small field in Mexico. There they would change the registration number and fly the plane to Europe via America and Canada. Gaunt said he had a buyer in Ireland who would pay double what he'd given for it."

"What went wrong?"

"Gaunt got drunk one night and disclosed that there was better than a half a million in uncut emeralds hidden on board and that Vogel was going to make a fortune."

"So your husband decided to cut himself in?"

She stared at us tragically. "I know it was wrong, but we'd had a lot of bad luck. I was working in London while his mother looked after the two boys. Things were very difficult."

"And Vogel agreed to pay more?"

"He had to. Jack was promised twenty-five thousand pounds and he refused to fly until it was paid over to me in London."

"He drove a hard bargain."

She gave a little shrug. "They didn't have much choice."

"And you didn't mind where the money came from?" Ilana said.

"There are worse things than smuggling." She sighed. "Or at least that's what I tried to tell myself. It was me he was thinking of, remember. Me and the boys."

They say it only takes one final straw and that was it for me. I clapped her ironically. "Slow curtain to cheers from the audience."

"For God's sake, give her a break, Joe," Desforge said. "Mrs. Kelso's had just about all she can take for one night."

"I applaud your sentiments," I said, "but just let's get one thing straight, shall we? She isn't Mrs. Kelso."

There was the kind of silence you get just after one clap of thunder when you're waiting for the next. Desforge stared at me in bewilderment and Sarah Kelso looked like a hunted animal who has just found the last route to freedom closed.

Ilana leaned forward, a slight frown on her face. "Just what are you getting at?" she demanded softly.

"It's quite simple really." I opened my arms wide. "Meet Jack Kelso."

CHAPTER FIFTEEN

It had all started with Jean Latouche, a barrel-chested French-Canadian bush pilot with the loudest laugh I've ever heard and a ragged black beard. He was a sort of twentieth century *voyageur* who used a floatplane instead of a canoe. From what I'd heard, he had the best part of a couple of hundred thousand dollars put away against his old age and a small portion of that had been earned flying in partnership with me on freight contracts to oil survey outfits in up-country Newfoundland.

That year the season had finished in Greenland by the last week in September as far as I was concerned, and I had flown over to Canada to see if I could pick up some extra cash before the snows came. I didn't have much luck, which was a pity, because although I'd managed to save twelve thousand dollars over the season as a whole, I was still on the books of the Silver Shield Finance Company of Toronto for sixteen thousand against the Otter. Not that they were going to cut my throat over it. I'd already paid off more than I needed to according to our agreement, but it was a big disappointment. I'd hoped to start the next season clean with the Otter bought and paid for.

I hung around Goose Bay for three days but nothing seemed to be happening so that I was glad of the work when a couple of geologists chartered me for a one way flight to a small airstrip west of Michikamau Lake called Carson Meadows. It was the sort of trip that netted me more than a couple of hundred dollars after expenses and I was sitting at the bar in the town's one and only hotel drinking black coffee and contemplating the future with foreboding when Jean Latouche came in.

He must have been at least fifty and wore flying boots and a great shaggy sheepskin coat that reached his knees. He dropped his duffle bag against the wall and advanced on me, hand outstretched.

"Eh, Joe, how goes it? You have a good season over there?"

"It could have been worse," I said. "It could also have been a damned sight better. How about you?"

"You know me, Joe. A crust, a jug of wine. I don't ask much."

"Like hell you don't," I commented sourly. "Where is it to be this winter? The Bahamas again or are you going to Tahiti this time?"

"You're beginning to sound bitter in your old age," he said. "What's wrong?"

"I'm tired, that's all. Tired of running round this God-forsaken country looking for work when there isn't any to be had."

He swallowed the cognac he'd ordered from the barman and asked for another. "Maybe you ain't been asking in the right places."

I looked at him hopefully. "Look, Jean, if you know of something then say the good word for God's sake."

"Don't get so excited, you probably won't be interested anyway. I know I wasn't. I was in Grant Bay yesterday. I met a fella there called Gaunt—Marvin Gaunt. He had a Heron fitted with auxiliary tanks. He's looking for someone to fly it to Ireland with him."

"What happened to his pilot?"

"He flew it in from Toronto himself in easy stages. He just isn't good enough to take on the Atlantic on his own, that's all."

"What's he offering?"

"A thousand dollars plus the return fare."

"Why didn't you take it?"

"I just didn't like the smell." He tapped his nose, a wise look on his face. "I've been around too long, Joe."

"You think he's up to no good?"

"I don't just think it—I know it." He got to his feet and clapped me on the shoulder. "No, it isn't for you, that one, Joe. Anyway, I've got to be on my way. Got a flight to the coast at noon. See you around."

I didn't, because he was killed a month later trying to land at Gander in a fog so thick you couldn't see your hand in front of your face, but I wasn't to know that as I sat there in that quiet little bar, brooding over my coffee or what was left of it, thinking about Marvin Gaunt and his Heron. A good aircraft, but he'd need those auxiliary tanks fitted to get her across the big pond. Still, with that done, it was a piece of cake and a thousand dollars was a thousand dollars. I paid for my coffee, and hurried back to the airstrip.

*

Grant Bay was a couple of hundred miles south of Goose and had been constructed to serve the local town and mining interests in the area. As I flew in, it was raining heavily and I wondered what Gaunt was doing there instead of some place like Gander in Newfoundland. It didn't make too much sense, not if he was really looking for a pilot.

There was a small tower, half a dozen hangars and three runways. I got permission to land, put the Otter down and parked beside the first hangar. I had a look inside all of them on the way down, but there was no sign of the Heron.

I found it in the open on the other side of the hangars, standing forlornly in the heavy rain. I walked round it slowly and paused, fascinated. On that side the Canadian registration number painted on the fuselage was crumbling at the edges in the heavy rain. I rubbed some more away with my fingers, just enough to confirm that there had been a previous registration, now painted over, which was very, very interesting and seemed to indicate that Jean's assessment of Gaunt hadn't been too far out.

He was staying at the town's one hotel and I found him in his room, a tall, rather handsome Englishman with the sort of public school voice that was too good to be true. By the time I'd spoken to him for five minutes, I had him pegged as someone who'd climbed rather a long way up the ladder.

"Mr. Gaunt?" I said when he opened the door. "I heard you were looking for a pilot."

"Oh, yes," he said. "And where did you hear that?"

"Carson Meadows," I replied promptly. "Someone was talking in a bar there."

He stood back and I went in. It wasn't much of a room—the sort you'd expect to find in a place like that. A mahogany wardrobe, an old bed, a thinning carpet. He went to the dresser, took a half bottle of whisky from a drawer and got a glass from the washbasin.

"Join me?"

I shook my head and he poured himself one and looked me over. "You've got a licence of course?"

I nodded and took out my wallet. Nobody knew me in Grant Bay and in view of the circumstances it might be a good idea to keep it that way. The previous year

I'd flown for a Lebanese air freight firm as co-pilot to a Canadian called Jack Kelso. By flying standards he was an old man—fifty-three—and had lived hard all his life, so no one was particularly surprised when he went on a three-day drunk for the last time and died of a heart attack in Basra.

I was with him at the time and had the job of collecting his things together, not that it was really worthwhile because as far as anyone knew he didn't have a relative in the world. I came across his pilot's licence when I was throwing things away and had kept it ever since, more as a souvenir than anything else.

I took it from my wallet and gave it to Gaunt who examined it briefly, then handed it back. "That all seems to be in order, Mr. Kelso, I've got a Heron down there on the field that I bought cheap in Toronto. I flew her here myself in easy stages, but I'm not up to crossing the Atlantic on my own. I've got a buyer waiting in Ireland who'll double my money if I can get it there by the end of the week. Are you interested?"

"What does it pay?"

"A thousand and your return fare from Shannon."

"Four thousand," I said. "Four thousand and my return fare." He managed a look of blank amazement, but before he could say anything I added, "Of course you could wait another couple of days to see if anyone else turns up, but I doubt it. It's the wrong time in the season. Another thing, if that Heron stands out there much longer, the rain will wash the registration right off and then we'll all be able to see what it really is—or wouldn't that bother you?"

He took it right on the chin. "All right, Mr. Kelso, four thousand. Four thousand plus your return fare. I think we should do very well together."

"In cash," I said. "Before we leave."

"And when will that be?"

I'd already decided that I'd rather fly back to Goose and leave the Otter there. I could always get a lift back in the mail plane if nothing else was available.

"If the met report is satisfactory we could take off to-morrow afternoon," I said. "Does that suit you?"

"Couldn't be better. I'll have her checked over in the morning."

"You do that."

I left him there and went back to the airstrip, already half-regretting my decision, but it was too late for that kind of talk now. I'd said I was going and go I would. The money would solve my personal problems nicely and any stray thoughts about what Gaunt might be up to I pushed firmly into the back of my mind and closed the door. I didn't want to know. As far as I was con-cerned, it was just another charter or at least, that's what I tried to tell myself.

*

It was still raining as I prepared for take-off on the following afternoon, but the met report for the crossing was pretty good. There was no customs' control to pass through as it was a passage out and at a field like Grant Bay, formalities were cut to the minimum. Gaunt han-dled all the documentation and even the two mechanics who tuned the engines for take-off didn't get a clear look at my face, which suited me down to the ground.

Gaunt had my money waiting for me in crisp new hundred dollar bills and I slipped them into an envelope I'd already prepared and posted it to myself, care of General Delivery at Goose Bay. So everything seemed to be taken care of. I'd calculated that we should get about half-way across on the normal tanks before having to switch to the auxiliaries and was sitting in the pilot's seat doing an instrument check when Gaunt joined me.

He was wearing a newish one-piece flying suit and looked extremely cheerful as he strapped himself into the co-pilot's seat.

"Ready to go?" I said.

"Whenever you like. There's just one thing." He handed me a map that had been neatly clipped to one of the chart boards. "If you have a look at that you'll see that I've changed our destination."

The course he'd charted ran north-west from Grant Bay in a dead straight line, cutting across the tip of Greenland and finishing at Reykjavik in Iceland, a flight of about sixteen hundred miles.

"What's the idea?" I said.

He took an envelope from one of his pockets and passed it across. "There's another thousand in there—all right?"

They were just as new as the others and just as attractive. I slipped them back into the envelope and put it into the inside pocket of my flying jacket. After all, what did it matter to me? Reykjavik or Shannon. It was all the same.

He smiled contentedly. "We won't bother informing the tower of our change of destination, old man. I'd much rather they still booked us down as being en route to the old country."

"You're the boss," I said and taxied out into the runway.

It was still raining as we took off and the sky was as heavy as lead, but I remembered the forecast and wasn't worried. I didn't alter course until we were well out to sea. The plane handled nicely—very nicely indeed and somewhere on the far horizon, the edge of a cloud was touched with light. I sat back, my hands steady on the controls and started to enjoy myself.

*

A couple of hours later and five hundred miles out, I'd had my fun. I handed over to Gaunt who hadn't had much to say for himself and went to the lavatory in the tail of the plane. That's when I got my first big shock because when I opened the door there was a man in there dressed like one of the mechanics at Grant Bay. In other circumstances it could have had its funny side, but there was nothing humorous about the Luger automatic pistol he was holding in his right hand.

"Surprise, surprise! Actually I was just about to look you up." The Luger moved so that the muzzle pointed in the general region of my stomach. "Shall we see what dear old Marvin has to say for himself?"

The same throwaway public school voice as Gaunt's but this one was for real, I was sure of that and there was a glint in his eye that said he meant business.

"I wouldn't know what all this is about," I said, "but I'd be obliged if you'd point that thing somewhere else. Gaunt's doing his best, but I'm the pilot really and we don't want any nasty accidents this far out over the Atlantic."

"My dear chap I could fly this crate to China and back with one hand tied behind my back."

I had the sort of feeling you get in the bar at the Royal Aero Club when some bore with a moustache a yard long takes a deep breath and you know that a second later you're going to get summer 1940, Biggin Hill and what it was really like doing a dozen sorties a day in a Spitfire.

I moved back through the body of the plane and

opened the cabin door. Gaunt turned to grin at me and the smile faded from his face.

"Harrison," he said blankly.

"In person, old man." Harrison tapped me on the shoulder with the Luger. "Sit down and take over."

Gaunt had gone very pale, but he didn't look as if he had lost control. In fact I could almost hear the wheels turning inside as he looked for some way out of this.

"Would someone kindly tell me what all this is about?" I said.

Harrison shook his head. "Not your affair, old man. All I want from you are a few facts and figures. How long is the course you've plotted from Grant Bay to Shannon?"

I glanced across at Gaunt who nodded. "We're not going to Shannon," I said. "Our destination is Reykjavik in Iceland."

"Well, bless my soul," he said. "That is a turn-up for the book. How far have we come?"

"Just over six hundred."

He smiled brightly. "Ah, well, Iceland will suit me just as well as anywhere else." He looked down at Gaunt. "You know, Marvin, you were really very stupid. All I wanted was my share."

"All right, all right!" Gaunt raised a hand quickly as if to shut him up. "No need to advertise. We can discuss it elsewhere."

Harrison backed out of the cabin and Gaunt followed him, closing the door. They were out there for a good five minutes and talked all the time, but I wasn't able to catch what they were saying. The shots, when they came, sounded remote and far away. There were two very close together, a short pause and then three more, two of which passed through the door splintering the windscreen.

I put the automatic pilot in control and unstrapped myself quickly. As I got to my feet and turned, the door burst open and Gaunt fell into my arms. I pushed him down into the other seat and he clawed at my jacket as I tried to unfasten his flying suit at the neck. And then blood erupted from his mouth and he lolled back, his head turning sideways, eyes fixed and staring.

Harrison was lying just inside the main cabin, face-down and when I turned him over, he was already dead, shot twice through the body. So there I was, up to my neck in trouble, two dead bodies on my hands, mixed up in something that was obviously far more serious than I'd ever appreciated

I went down to the galley, poured hot coffee from a Thermos and lit a cigarette. What was I going to do, that was the thing? I could always drop them both over the side, but that still meant I had to land somewhere and the plane would take a hell of a lot of explaining away because even if I just dumped it there would still be enquiries and that was the last thing I wanted. Of course, the ideal solution would have been to send the damned thing down to the bottom of the Atlantic with both of them inside, but that wouldn't do me much good. There was a variation on that theme, of course. Find a suitable piece of wilderness and bale out leaving the Heron to come down the hard way. With the additional petrol she was carrying in the auxiliary tanks she would go up like a torch.

What I needed sounded like an impossibility. The sort of area so sparsely populated that the crash would pass unnoticed and yet so close to some sort of civilisation that I would have a fair chance of walking out.

The solution, when it came, was so simple that I almost laughed out loud. I hurried back to the pilot's cabin, sat down in my seat again and reached for the chart. I found what I was looking for straight away—the Julianehaab Bight on the southwest coast of Greenland and the little fishing village of Sandvig, the fjord on which it stood cutting inland through the mountains to the icecap beyond.

That icecap was one of the most desolate places on God's earth. Through the years many planes had disappeared over it without trace. The Heron would be just one more and in any case, the official view when it failed to show at Shannon, would be that it was at the bottom of the Atlantic somewhere.

I calculated the distance to the coast carefully. Four hundred and fifty miles to go and according to the dial, there was enough fuel left in the tanks for approximately another five hundred miles. It couldn't have been more perfect. All I had to do was put it on automatic pilot and jump without switching the auxiliary tanks through. The plane would fly on perhaps another fifty miles, but when the fuel gave out it would nosedive, exploding like a bomb on impact.

The only tricky bit was going to be the jump, but that was a calculated risk I'd just have to take. I lit a cigarette, reached for the automatic pilot control and found myself looking Gaunt straight in the face. It wasn't very pleasant and I pushed him away to the other side of the seat, switched off the automatic pilot and took control again. All I needed now was a plausible story for my good friend Olaf Rasmussen when I walked in on him at his farm above Sandvig. But that shouldn't prove too difficult. There was a road of sorts linking Frederiksborg and Sandvig. I could say I'd been on the hunting trip I'd talked about all season, but had been too busy to take. That I'd had some kind of accident and lost all my gear. I had the bare bones of a story. Now I started to concentrate on making it sound convincing.

*

I brought the plane in low over the sea and took her up to three thousand as land appeared and beyond, through the harsh white moonlight, the Greenland ice-cap gleamed like a string of pearls.

East from Cape Desolation the Julianehaab Bight was full of smoky mist indicating no wind to speak of and certainly nothing more than five knots, which was something. At least it gave me the chance of dropping into the valley at the head of the fjord. Not much of a one, but better than staying here.

It was cold in the cabin with the night wind streaming in through the splintered windscreen and the lighted dials on the instrument panel were confusing in their multiplicity, occasionally merging into a meaningless blur.

And then, on the far side of the mist the waters of the fjord gleamed silvery white in the intense light and the strange twisted moonscape rolled towards the ice-cap, every feature etched razor-sharp.

It was time to go. I reduced speed, put the auto pilot in control and unbuckled my safety belt. When I turned Gaunt's body had slid round again so that he seemed to be staring at me, mouth slightly parted as if he would speak, head disembodied in the light from the instrument panel.

I moved into the darkness of the main cabin, stumbling across Harrison's body so that I fell to one knee and my outstretched hand touched his ice-cold face. God knows why, but at that moment I suddenly became desperately afraid and lurched through the darkness and clawed at the quick release handles on the exit hatch. It fell away into the night and I stepped into space without hesitation, aware of the intense cold, feeling strangely free. I seemed to somersault in slow motion and for a single moment saw the plane above me in the night drifting steadily eastwards like some dark ghost and then I reached for the ring to open my chute.

For a moment it seemed to stick and my throat went dry. I tugged again with all my strength. I still continued to fall, turning over and then, quite suddenly, I heard what at the right moment is the most reassuring sound in the world—the crack of a chute opening above your head, blossoming like a white flower as the air fills it. I started to drift down into the hills at the head of the fjord.

CHAPTER SIXTEEN

Rain drummed against the window and I peered out into the gathering darkness.

"What happened after you landed?" Desforge asked.

I turned to face them. "I had a rather enjoyable twelve-mile hike by moonlight. When I walked in on Olaf Rasmussen I told him I'd been on a hunting trip in the mountains from Frederiksborg. That I'd managed to scramble clear when my jeep had gone over the edge of the road on a washed-out section taking all my gear with it. That sort of thing happens all the time in country like this. He didn't question it for a moment. The following day I got a lift to Frederiksborg in a fishing boat. From there I flew to Newfoundland in one of the Catalina flying boats that East Canada Airways use on the coastal run. They always get out before the ice starts."

Sarah Kelso sat on the edge of the bed, her handkerchief screwed up into a ball, her face drained of all colour. Desforge turned slowly, looked down at her. "You certainly fooled me, angel. Who are you, anyway?"

"Does that matter now?" she said.

"No, I suppose it doesn't."

He poured himself another drink and I pulled a chair

forward and sat down in front of her. "Shall we have the truth now?"

"All right," she said wearily. "What do you want to know?"

"Let's start with the emeralds. Who did they belong to originally?"

"The International Investment Company of Brazil. They were a plane shipment to São Paulo from somewhere in the interior. Gaunt hi-jacked them with some local help and Harrison was waiting to fly him out."

"And Vogel was behind the whole deal?"

"That's right."

"Where did you fit in?"

She shrugged. "I work for Vogel—have done for years."

"When the plane went missing what was Vogel's reaction?"

"Oh, he accepted it completely. Said it was just one of those things."

"Didn't he worry about the mysterious Mr. Kelso?"

She shook her head. "Not particularly. Harrison frequently used another identity and in any case, there was nowhere they could have gone—not without Vogel getting some sort of word. Another thing, there was always the insurance which was better than nothing."

"You mean he actually had the company pay out?"

"Why not? It was a legitimate claim. In any case, you don't seem to realise. He *is* the London and Universal Insurance Company."

Desforge poured himself another drink. "From what you say, Joe, it looks as if Gaunt was trying to pull a fast one and Harrison simply caught up with him."

I nodded and said to Sarah Kelso, "It was a neat idea to pass you off as Kelso's widow. Tell me something—

the dental record and signet ring? Who did they really belong to?"

"Gaunt," she said.

I glanced up at Desforge. "Simple when you know how and no one would think to query the cause of death, not with the state those two bodies were in."

He shook his head in bewilderment. "One thing I don't understand—what happened to the emeralds?"

I told him about the package Gudrid had addressed to herself at Sandvig and he whistled softly. "That must be just about the most ironic twist of all. Isn't this about the time when Simonsen should be taking a hand?"

"He's at a fishing village a hundred miles up the coast from here at the moment," I said. "Won't be back till tomorrow afternoon. In fact he's expecting me to pick him up."

"And by that time you'll be long gone I suppose."

"I expect so."

I moved to the window and looked outside. The fog was thickening but the rain had slackened off considerably. When I turned, Ilana was standing a couple of feet away. Her eyes were unnaturally large and her skin seemed to have tightened over her cheekbones, aging her considerably.

"Did you mean that?" she demanded. "About clearing out before the storm breaks."

"It would seem the sensible thing to do," I said. "If I stay, anything could happen after what I did."

"Tell me something. If you'd kept quiet would anyone have known that Gaunt and Harrison had been shot to death?"

Desforge cut in quickly. "She's got a point there, Joe. From what you told us those bodies must have been in a hell of a state."

"Then why didn't you keep quiet," she said. "With any kind of luck you needn't have been involved at all."

I'd been asking myself the same question for some time now without coming up with an answer that made any kind of sense. "God knows," I said. "Maybe I have a deathwish or something or perhaps I just can't keep out of trouble."

She smiled gently. "You won't run, Joe. It's not in your nature—not any more."

And she was right, I knew that the moment she said it. The days when I turned back on any part of life and simply walked away from it were in the past.

I grinned. "All right, what do I do now? Sally forth into the night and capture Vogel and Stratton single-handed?"

Desforge went to the window and peered out. "I wouldn't have thought there was much point. I mean where in the hell can they go in a pea-souper like this."

He was right, of course. There was simply no way out until the weather cleared and at sea that schooner of Da Gama's wouldn't last half a day with the Danish Navy corvette that had been doing coastal survey work out of Godthaab on its tail. I suddenly realised that the whole thing was as good as over. Vogel and Stratton didn't stand a chance, hadn't from the moment Arnie had been murdered. That had really been a very stupid thing to do. Surprising really, for someone like Vogel, but on the other hand a man was only as good as the people who worked for him.

"What are you going to do about Arnie?" Ilana said.

I shrugged. "There isn't much we can do, is there? Better to leave things exactly as they are for Simonsen to see tomorrow. I think that's what he'd want."

There was a knock on the door and when I opened it, Gudrid was standing there. Her face was blotched and swollen with weeping, but otherwise she seemed to be in control of herself.

"Mr. Martin, I wonder if you'd do me a great favour?"

"If I can."

"I'd like to charter your plane. Could you fly me down to Sandvig first thing in the morning? I want to get away from here—right away."

"Olaf Simonsen might not be too happy about that when he gets back tomorrow afternoon," I said.

"If he wants me, he can come to Sandvig for me." She clutched my arm. "Please, Mr. Martin."

I nodded slowly. "All right, Gudrid, but it all depends on the weather, remember. You'd better pray for the fog to lift."

"Thank you, Mr. Martin." There was real relief on her face as she moved to the door and then she hesitated and turned slowly. "What was in the package Arnie gave me, Mr. Martin?"

"Emeralds, Gudrid," I said. "A fortune in emeralds. He would have been rich beyond his wildest dreams. Enough to go to anyone's head."

"And that's why he was murdered." I nodded. "Do you know who did it?"

"That's for the police to decide. Let's say we have a fair idea. Why do you ask?"

"It doesn't matter," she said calmly. "After all, nothing can bring him back now, can it?"

I watched her go and swallowed hard. Another of those times when I could have done with a drink. As I turned, Sarah Kelso got up wearily. Her eyes had sunk into their sockets, her face was pinched and drawn. I remembered the supremely beautiful woman I'd met only three nights ago and could detect not the slightest resemblance.

192

"If no one has any objection, I think I'd like to go to bed," she said.

Desforge looked at me, compassion in his eyes. "Let her go, Joe. After all, where can she run to?"

Which was true enough and I nodded without speaking. She went out, closing the door softly behind her.

"And now what?" Desforge said.

I suddenly realised I was hungry and glanced at my watch. It was just after ten. "Still time for a late dinner if anyone feels like joining me?"

"And that's the best idea yet," Desforge said. "Just give me time to change," and he went into the bedroom.

I turned to Ilana and held out my hands. She hesitated before taking them. "What's this for?"

"I just wanted to thank you," I said. "For straightening me out."

"Oh, that!" she smiled faintly. "I wonder if you'll feel the same way when the court has finished with you."

"Very civilised people the Danes," I said. "Finest prisons in the world or didn't you know?"

"I always thought that was Sweden?"

"Now you've got me worried." I pulled her into my arms and kissed her.

*

In view of the circumstances it may sound macabre to say that I ate a hearty meal, but the truth was that I'd only had a sandwich since flying in from Sandvig that morning. Desforge wasn't far behind me, but Ilana contented herself with coffee and watched us eat.

We sat in the bar for an hour afterwards and I made do with cigarettes and more coffee while Desforge consumed his usual quantity of alcohol. At one stage in the conversation he suddenly pointed out that by flying Gudrid down to Sandvig I'd be able to return with the emeralds, which for some reason hadn't occurred to me before. Beyond that, we didn't really discuss what had happened, but it was there just the same beneath the surface of things and our general conversation was disjointed and without any real pattern to it.

It was half past eleven when we went upstairs. I asked Ilana to check on Sarah Kelso and Desforge and I went on to his room. Ilana joined us within a couple of minutes.

"She's sleeping, which seems the sensible thing to do. It's been a long and interesting day so I think I'll turn in. I'll see you in the morning."

Desforge was pouring himself a drink, his back to us and she looked up at me very deliberately as if waiting for something. I did the only thing I could think of which was to put an arm around her and walk her to the door. I kissed her briefly. She had expected more, so much was obvious and I couldn't imagine what it might be. There was something close to disappointment in her eyes when she went out.

I turned and found Desforge looking at me gravely. "You want to watch yourself there, Joe," he said. "The hooks are out."

"You think so?"

"I know so. I've seen it all before. Why waste your time?"

There was a kind of malice underlying what he had said, an edge of viciousness that wasn't really necessary. It was almost as if he hated her now and in view of her father's attitude towards financing the picture, that might well be true. Or perhaps he simply resented her going elsewhere? The old lion still trying to hang on to what was his.

I didn't pursue it and he let it drop and suggested a hand of cards. We played poker, blackjack, a few hands of whist and ended up with a diabolical little game called Slippery Sam that I hadn't played since my navy days. He took a little over two hundred dollars off me and by three-thirty I'd had enough.

I left him and went along to my bedroom. I didn't feel tired and I flung myself on the bed and stared up at the ceiling, thinking about it all.

A moment later the door opened and Desforge came in. "She's gone," he said simply.

"Sarah Kelso?"

He nodded. "I've just looked in."

His reasons were pretty obvious, but that didn't concern me now and I swung my feet to the floor and got up. "Have you checked with Ilana?"

"First place I looked, but there's no sign of her there. Ilana's getting dressed. She'll be here in a minute."

I left him there and went along the corridor and knocked on Gudrid's door. When she opened it I saw with some surprise, that she was still dressed.

"Oh, it's you, Mr. Martin." She nodded towards a couple of suitcases on the bed. "I couldn't sleep so I've been packing."

"I want you to do something for me," I said. "Mrs. Kelso seems to have disappeared. Check with the rest of the night staff. See what you can find out without making too much of a fuss."

She nodded breathlessly, her face white and excited and I left her there, went down the back stairs and let myself out of the yard door. The hotel had two Land-rovers which were kept in a garage across the yard. One was obviously in use so I took the other and drove away as quickly as the fog would allow.

The road down to the harbour was deserted and when I reached the canning factory I parked the Landrover and went the rest of the way to the jetty on foot. I was wasting my time, of course. Incredible as it seemed in view of the weather conditions, Da Gama's schooner had disappeared as completely as if it had never existed.

*

It was just after four as I drove back into the yard at the rear of the hotel and already dawn was seeping through the curtain of fog so that I could see the outlines of buildings clearly.

When I went up to Desforge's room, I found Gudrid and Ilana waiting for me, Desforge pacing up and down restlessly, the inevitable glass in his hand.

He swung round as I walked in. "Where in the hell have you been?"

"Down to the jetty to check on that schooner of Da Gama's. It's gone, taking them all with it presumably. They must be raving mad. There are icebergs all over the place out there."

"You've got it all wrong, Joe," Desforge said. "You'd better sit down and hear what Gudrid has to say."

"I had a word with the night clerk," Gudrid began. "It seems Mrs. Kelso had a telephone call at eleven o'clock. The girl says it was a man and the conversation was in English. Later, Mrs. Kelso phoned down and asked if there was a map available covering the area of the Frederiksborg-Sandvig road. One was sent up to her."

"Anything else?"

"Yes, the night porter was putting out kitchen refuse just before midnight when he saw Mr. Vogel and Mr. Stratton come into the yard with a third man he didn't know. They took one of the Landrovers from the garage, but he didn't think anything of that as they are hired out regularly to hotel guests. As he was going back into the kitchen, Mrs. Kelso came out of the back door and joined them. He said that Mr. Vogel kissed her, then they all got into the Landrover and drove away together."

"She's certainly an expert at changing sides," Ilana said bitterly.

"Still think they've gone off on the schooner, Joe?" Desforge demanded.

"No, I suppose it's pretty obvious what they're up to," I said. "They can reach Sandvig by road in six hours. I know that because I've done it myself. In fact, with luck on their side, they could be there by five or five-thirty."

"Is there a telephone?" Ilana asked.

Gudrid shook her head. "There's a radio at the trading post, but the factor doesn't live on the premises. He has a farm up on the hill. He opens the post at eight a.m. We could send a message then."

"About three hours too late," Desforge said.

Ilana frowned in bewilderment. "But the whole thing is so pointless, can't they see that? Where on earth do they go from Sandvig?"

Which was exactly what I'd been thinking myself and there seemed to be only one obvious solution. "They've probably arranged a rendezvous with the schooner."

"But what if it doesn't make it?" Desforge said. "You said yourself they must be insane to take her out in this fog."

"At this stage in the game they don't have much option. And there's always another possibility. The airport at Narssarssuaq. That's only a couple of hours from Sandvig by motorboat and plenty of fishermen to take

197

them if the price was right. They could have their pick of flights to Europe via Iceland or the other way to Canada or the States."

"So—it looks as if nothing can stop them."

I shook my head and what I said next shocked even me. "That isn't quite true. I could be at Sandvig in forty minutes in the Otter, remember."

"In this fog?" Desforge laughed abruptly. "Who are you trying to kid. You can't see more than twenty yards in front of you. You wouldn't even get off the water."

"Taking off isn't the problem. It's landing at the other end that I don't fancy. I don't know whether you noticed, but one side of Sandvig fjord consists of a thousand-foot wall of rock."

Desforge shook his head. "Listen, Joe, I've got a licence—I can fly myself. God knows, I've done enough of it in pictures, but a flight like that is strictly for a nice big studio mock-up with the wind machines howling and the cameras just out there beyond the smoke. People don't do things like that in real life."

That's all it took. Looking back now, I wonder if he was simply being extremely clever and goading me to do what I'd never seriously intended. If so, he succeeded admirably. I don't know what came over me, but I was suddenly seized by an excitement so intense that it was impossible to handle.

As if he sensed what I was thinking, he said gently, "You'd never make it, Joe."

"You're probably right," I said. "But I know one thing. I'm going to have a damned good try."

Ilana's face was pale, her eyes burning, but I held the door open and was away before she could say anything.

*

I went to my room and changed into flying gear. By the time I was ready to go some of my initial enthusiasm had evaporated, that was true, but I hadn't changed my mind, and gripped by a strange fatalism I went down the back stairs and crossed the yard to the garage.

I dropped my bag into the rear of the Landrover and paused. Gudrid's two suitcases were already in and Desforge's Winchester in its worn case. I turned and the three of them stepped out of the shadows.

"Rotten morning," Desforge said brightly.

"What exactly do you think you're playing at?" I demanded.

Desforge seemed to give the matter due consideration.

"Let's just say we're tired of the tedium of everyday life."

"You must be raving mad, all of you," I began and Ilana simply brushed past me and climbed into the Landrover.

*

I borrowed a dinghy with an outboard motor and checked my run from the end of the slipway out there into the fjord. It was all clear and when I returned, Desforge had the engine warming up for me.

I strapped myself into the pilot's seat and turned to look at the two girls.

"Better close your eyes tight. This is going to be pretty hair-raising."

That was the understatement of the age. To plunge headlong into that grey wall was probably the most psychologically terrifying thing I'd ever done in my life, but I held on, giving her full throttle, lifting her at the earliest possible moment.

Twenty seconds later we climbed out of the fog and turned south.

*

It was certainly a spectacular flight. The fog covered the sea below like smoke in a valley, and to the east the peaks of the coastal range pushed through it majestically, an unforgettable sight.

"It doesn't look too good, does it?" Desforge said and strangely enough there was a smile on his face and his eyes sparkled.

"It's what things are like at Sandvig that matters," I told him grimly.

"Worried?" There was a kind of challenge in his voice.

"To be absolutely precise, frightened to death. If conditions are anything like this at the other end, you'd all better start praying."

Gudrid turned pale and gripped the arm of her seat tightly. Ilana offered her a cigarette and said brightly, "He also likes to pull the wings off flies."

"Thanks for the vote of confidence," I said and concentrated on my flying.

There was a kind of perverse comfort in having managed to transfer a little of my own fear on to someone else and for the next half hour I simply sat there, trimming the controls when necessary in a sort of reflex action, thinking about the whole strange business.

From Vogel's point of view, the strength of his plan had been its essential simplicity, but that had also constituted its greatest weakness. A few careful steps across the tightrope and he would have been home and dry. Unfortunately for him there were two things he hadn't reckoned with—my own existence and Sarah Kelso's treachery.

Which made me think of Arnie and for a moment I saw him again, lying there behind the couch, blood on the wall. The most stupid and senseless part of the whole affair. Poor Arnie. What was it he had said? *Take whatever is going because you can never count on tomorrow.* Perhaps he'd had something there after all.

I came back to myself with a start as Desforge gripped my arm and when I looked down, I could see the fog ending abruptly as if someone had sliced it neatly across with a knife and we flew into heavy drenching rain, the sea clear beyond.

From then on the whole thing was a bit of an anticlimax. Certainly visibility in the fjord when we reached it was considerably reduced by the heavy rain, and a tracer of mist obscured Rasmussen's farm up on the hill, but the landing presented no difficulty at all.

I swung in a wide circle, chose a course parallel with the great rock face on the other side of the fjord and two hundred yards away from it, and put the Otter down.

CHAPTER SEVENTEEN

"So, here we are then," I said as we drifted to a halt.

I could have sworn there was an expression of disappointment on Desforge's face, but he forced a grin. "Rotten third act, Joe. Anti-climax."

I turned and glanced at the women. "Okay back there?"

Gudrid had colour in her cheeks again and Ilana smiled, "As ever was."

I started to light a cigarette and Desforge held up his hand. "I thought I heard something."

I opened the window and rain drifted in and we sat there in silence, the only noise the occasional slap of a small wave against the floats. Desforge told Ilana to pass him the Winchester and he started to unfasten the straps on the gun case as I leaned out of the window.

There was the muffled put-put of a small outboard motor somewhere near at hand and then a voice called in Danish and I relaxed. A small dinghy coasted out of the rain, Bergsson the trading post factor sitting in the stern. He cut the motor and drifted in beside the float.

He grinned up, his beard spangled with tiny beads of moisture. "Morning, Joe, you're lucky. Half an hour ago the fjord was choked with fog, then the rain came in and cleared it all away."

"It was pretty bad when we left Frederiksborg," I said.

Gudrid leaned forward. "Good morning, Mr. Bergsson. How is my grandfather?"

"Fine, Miss Rasmussen. I was with him last on the day before yesterday."

He was obviously astonished to see her, but before he could carry on I said quickly, "And not since then? Wasn't there some mail for him on the boat yesterday afternoon?"

"I wouldn't know," he said. "The boat was delayed by fog and didn't get in till late last night, so I haven't got around to sorting out the mail yet. It's still in the bag at the store."

"That's fine," I said. "When you open up I think you'll find a package addressed to Gudrid care of her grandfather. We can save you a trip."

"But I don't understand." He was by now completely bewildered.

"You don't need to. Just turn the boat round and we'll follow you in."

He gave up, shrugged and went back to the stern of his dinghy. While he busied himself starting the motor I gave Desforge and Ilana the substance of what had been said.

"What happens when you've got your hands on the sparklers?" Desforge asked.

"We'll borrow Bergsson's old jeep and ride up to Olaf Rasmussen's place and warn him what's in the offing. We should be able to provide some sort of reception committee for Vogel and his friends. Olaf usually has half a dozen Eskimo shepherds around the place and they can revert to the ways of their forefathers awfully fast if anyone starts baring his teeth at them."

Gudrid shook her head. "But my grandfather will be on his own at the moment, Mr. Martin, surely you haven't forgotten. At this time in the season the shepherds will be away in the hills searching out the sheep, preparing them for the drive down to the valley." She turned to Ilana. "Four more weeks—five at the most and winter begins and always so quickly that we are caught unawares."

"All right, so we go up and get him out of there before they arrive."

I started the engine and Desforge patted the barrel of the Winchester. "I could certainly give them one hell of a surprise with this from the loft of that barn. Hell, they'd be sitting ducks when they drove into the farmyard."

With a cigarette dangling from the corner of his mouth, the Winchester across his knees and the tousled hair falling across his forehead, the reckless gleam in his eyes, he looked too much like a still from one of his own pictures for comfort.

I said shortly, "Don't be bloody stupid, Jack, we aren't on Stage 6 now. This is for real. People die, they don't just pick themselves up off the floor at the end and take a vacation till the next script comes along."

He blazed with anger, hands tightening on the gun. "I wasn't play-acting in the rear turret of that B29, you limey bastard. Thirty-one scripts and then I got a slug through the thigh and that was for real. I got medals, baby. What did they ever give you?"

I could have said that I had medals too, whatever that proved, only in my case I'd been only too anxious to forget the whole stupid senseless business as soon as possible, but I didn't. There wouldn't have been any point. I don't even think he'd have understood what I was trying to say. I had a brief glimpse of Ilana's face out of the corner of my eye, shocked and for some inexplicable reason, frightened and I pushed up the throttle slowly and went after the dinghy.

*

The constraint between Desforge and myself overshadowed everything, diminishing even the excitement of the moment when Bergsson found the package in the mailbag and passed it to Gudrid. She tore off the outer wrapping and disclosed a cardboard shoebox carefully sealed with Scotch tape.

"This is exactly as it was when Arnie gave it to me," she said.

I took out a clasp knife and cut round the lid quickly. It contained a grey canvas money belt, each separate pouch bulging. I opened one and spilled a couple of the uncut gems into the palm of my hand.

"So that's what they look like?" Desforge said.

I nodded. "Before the experts get to work on them." I replaced the stones in their pouch, buckled the belt around my waist and turned to Bergsson. "Is it all right if we borrow your jeep?"

"Certainly." He sensed that something unusual was going on, so much was obvious and added awkwardly, "Look, if there's anything I can do."

"I don't think so."

Desforge broke in harshly. "We're wasting time. Let's get out of here."

He stalked outside and I paused at the door beside Ilana. "What's eating him, for God's sake?"

She looked worried. "I don't know—sometimes he gets like this, nervous and irrational, flaring up into a sudden rage at nothing at all. Perhaps he needs a drink."

"More likely he's had too many for too long," I said sourly and went outside.

Desforge was sitting at the wheel of the jeep, the rifle beside him and he glared up at me belligerently. "Any objections?"

"Suit yourself."

I climbed into the rear seat. Ilana hesitated, obviously torn between us, but Gudrid solved the problem by getting into the passenger seat beside Desforge.

"Well make your mind up," he said irritably. "Are you coming or aren't you?"

She didn't reply—just got into the rear seat beside me and stared straight in front of her, hands tightly clasped as we drove away.

*

The rain was lifting a little now, not too much, but increasing visibility to fifty yards or so as we followed the winding dirt road up the hill. The slope below us dropped steeply to the fjord and was covered by alder scrub with here and there clumps of willow and birch up to ten feet high. On the right-hand side Iceland poppies showed scarlet amongst lichen covered rocks and there were alpines and saxifrage—even buttercups, so that it might have been the Tyrol on a misty morning after rain.

Desforge was driving too fast considering the conditions, but I was damned if I was going to tell him that. I didn't get much of a chance anyway because when we were about half-way up the hill, the hotel Landrover came round a bend and rushed towards us at what seemed a terrifying speed in those conditions.

There was a moment when everything seemed to stop, the whole scene frozen like a still picture and then Desforge swung the wheel of the old jeep without even attempting to brake and took the left-hand side of the track as the Landrover skidded to a halt. There couldn't have been more than a foot in it as we went by and our off-side rear wheel spun wildly, seeking a grip on thin air.

The jeep dipped sideways, spilling me over the edge and I tucked my head into my shoulder and yelled as I hit the dirt and rolled down the slope through the scrub.

As I scrambled to my feet, the jeep roared like an angry lion and regained the road in a shower of dirt and gravel and Desforge braked to a halt. Behind him the Landrover was already reversing and Stratton stood up and grabbed the edge of the windscreen, an automatic ready in his hand.

He loosed off a wild shot and I shouted. "For God's sake get moving. Get the women out of here. Make for the farm."

Desforge had enough sense not to argue and the jeep vanished into the rain as the Landrover braked to a halt above me. Stratton shouted something, but I couldn't catch what it was and then he jumped for the slope, landing thirty or forty feet above me in a shower of stones, the automatic ready in his right hand. As the Landrover took off after the jeep, I turned and ran for my life, ploughing through the alder head-down as he fired twice.

Branches whipped against my face as I scrambled through a grove of birches and then I stumbled and fell again, turning on my back and going down in the rain, riding a bank of scree in a long breathless slide that ended on a beach at the edge of the fjord.

I picked myself up and staggered along the shingle, collapsing into the temporary safety of a horseshoe of black rocks. For a moment only as I lay there I might have been a twelve-year-old lying on a Scottish shore on some forgotten morning, my face against the pebbles. And these were the same as they are on most beaches the world over. Typical chalcedony. Translucent red Carnelian, brown and red jasper, banded onyx and agate.

My fingers hooked into them and I lay there, hardly daring to breathe, listening for the sound of his pursuit, but there was nothing. Only the rustle of the wind as it moved down from the mountains pushing the rain before it and the quiet lapping of the water.

*

I waited five minutes and then moved along the shore to a point which was, as far as I could judge, directly beneath the farmhouse. I was pretty certain of my ground because at this point a great granite crag jutted from the hillside and I went up one side of it, making much faster time than I would had I stuck to the scrub.

At this height there was still some fog, but it was thinning rapidly now, swirling around me in strange, menacing shapes. My heart was pounding like a triphammer and there was blood in my mouth as I heaved myself over a shelf of rock and crouched on top of the crag. There was a grove of willow trees to the rear, the hillside lifting beyond to the south meadow below Rasmussen's farm.

I took a deep breath, pushed myself to my feet and started forward. At the same moment Stratton stood up from behind a boulder on the edge of the crag and said in a perfectly normal tone as if we were good friends who had somehow missed each other, "Ah, there you are, old chap."

As I started to turn he fired and the bullet shattered my wrist, the mark of a real pro who knows that a dying man might still be able to get a shot off at him, whereas a man with a broken wrist can't.

It's true what they say—when a bullet hits you, you don't feel any real pain, not at first. Only a sort of stunning blow delivered with the force of a blunt instrument swung by a rather large man, but the shock effect on the central nervous system is pretty considerable, driving the breath from your body like a kick in the belly.

I fell down, rolling on my face and fought for air. He stayed there at the edge, a slight fixed smile on his face. "I've been watching you for quite some time actually. Remarkable view from up here, even allowing for the fog." He shook his head. "You shouldn't have joined, old chap."

No shooting from the waist or any of that nonsense. His right hand swung up as he took deliberate aim and I screamed aloud, "Don't be a fool, Stratton, I know where the emeralds are!"

He hesitated fractionally, lowering the automatic and I scrambled to one knee, my left hand clawing into the dirt. As I came up, I let him have a handful right in the face. He ducked, an arm swinging up instinctively, took a short step backwards and went over the edge.

CHAPTER EIGHTEEN

The bones of my wrist had fragmented, I could tell that by the way they grated together when I wound a handkerchief around it in an attempt to stop the bleeding. It still wasn't hurting, not yet. That would come later and I tucked my hand inside my flying jacket and scrambled up the hill.

As I went through the fence at the top and started across the south meadow, a shot echoed flatly through the fog and two more sounded in reply. I put my head down and ran, ducking behind the grey stone wall that was the northern boundary, keeping to its shelter until I came to the farm.

Another shot sounded from the open door of the loft in the barn and two more were fired in reply from the house. I hurried back the way I had come and the moment the farmhouse was out of sight scrambled over the wall and approached from the rear.

The yard by the back door was deserted, but by this time I wasn't caring too much anyway because my wrist was beginning to hurt like hell, the pain crawling up my arm like some living thing.

I ran across the yard, head-down, expecting a bullet in the back at any second, but nothing happened and then I was at the door and it opened to receive me.

I didn't stop running until I cannoned into the wall

on the other side of the kitchen. Behind me, the door closed and a bolt was rammed home. When I turned, wiping sweat from my eyes with my left hand, Da Gama was standing facing me.

*

When I was pushed into the hall, I found Vogel crouched at the shattered window, a revolver in his hand, Sarah Kelso flattened against the wall beside him. Rasmussen lay on the table, eyes closed, blood on his head and Ilana and Gudrid were at his side.

Vogel looked me over calmly. "What happened to Stratton?"

"He tried to get down to the beach the hard way. I wouldn't count on seeing him again if I were you."

Another bullet shattered the window and everyone hit the floor. I crawled over to Ilana and held out my wrist. "Do what you can with this, will you? What happened here?"

She pulled a silk scarf from her neck and bound my wrist tightly. "When we got here Jack told us to get in the house. He said he was going to ambush them from the loft in the barn."

"What went wrong?"

"They came in the back way. Stupid, but there it is."

"This can't be his day for clear thinking," I said. "What about Rasmussen?"

"He tried to tackle Vogel and Da Gama hit him over the head with his gun."

Two more bullets smashed through the window, one of them ploughing into the floor and Gudrid screamed. Vogel turned towards me, his back to the wall as he reloaded his revolver, a smear of blood on his cheek.

"I think we've had enough of this nonsense. Come here, Miss Eytan." She hesitated and he nodded to Da

Gama who flung her forward. Vogel caught her by the hair, wrenched back her head and touched the barrel of his revolver to her temple. "Mr. Martin," he said evenly. "Go outside and tell Desforge I'll blow out his lady friend's brains if he doesn't come out of that barn within the next two minutes."

I didn't even get a chance to think it over because Da Gama dragged me to my feet, opened the door and shoved me outside. I dropped to one knee and a bullet chipped the wall beside the doorpost. From then on he obviously recognised me and I stumbled across the yard shouting his name.

As I ran into the entrance of the barn, he appeared at the edge of the loft above my head and standing up there in his old parka, the Winchester ready for action, he wasn't Jack Desforge any more. He was that other, legendary figure who had always seemed so much larger than life. As he dropped to the floor and moved towards me, I had the strange illusion that this was somehow a scene we had played many times before.

And when he spoke, it might have been dialogue straight off page fifty-seven of some script that had been specially written for him—the kind of film he had made a score of times.

"You don't look too good, kid. What happened?"

I told him about Stratton. "But that doesn't matter now. You've got to come in, Jack. Vogel swears he'll kill Ilana if you don't and I got a strong impression that he means it."

He nodded briefly, a strange remote look in his eyes as if his mind was elsewhere. "Okay, kid, if that's what you want. How do we know he won't pick us off on our way across the yard?"

"We find that out in next week's episode."

"I can't wait that long." He went out through the

open door in three or four quick strides and dropped the Winchester on the ground. "Okay, Vogel, you win."

For one wild moment I expected to see him go down under a fusillade of bullets. He stood there for a while, hands on hips as if waiting for something, and then the door across the yard opened and Vogel came out pushing Ilana in front of him.

Sarah Kelso followed, Da Gama at her heels, but there was no sign of Gudrid who had presumably stayed with the old man. We all met in the middle of the yard in a kind of awkward silence.

Vogel spoke first. "The emeralds, please, Mr. Martin."

I hesitated and Desforge said, and it was as if he was somehow in command, "Give them to him, Joe."

I unstrapped the belt and tossed it across. Vogel hefted it in his hand, face quite calm. "A long wait."

Ilana moved suddenly to join Desforge and me and swung to face the Austrian. "And what happens now, Mr. Vogel? Do we get what you gave Arnie Fassberg?"

Vogel smiled gently. "My dear Miss Eytan, like most determined sinners, I'm quite prepared to carry the burden of my own misdeeds, but I certainly object to being made responsible for someone else's. I don't know who killed the unfortunate Mr. Fassberg, but it certainly wasn't me or any of my associates."

There was no reason for him to lie, none at all and Ilana turned and stared at me blankly. "But who, Joe? Who else could it have been?"

"Only one person I can think of," I said. "The person who told him about the emeralds in the first place."

Sarah Kelso seemed to shrink visibly, the skin tightening across her cheeks, a hand going to her mouth involuntarily as she took a hurried step backwards. "Oh, no—never in a thousand years."

"But it had to be you," I said. "There is no one else."

For a long moment she seemed to be struck dumb and it was Desforge who spoke, his voice quiet and calm and very, very tired.

"Sure there was, kid, there was me. She found that letter at the Fredericsmut, remember? The one from Milt Gold. She knew I'd reached the end of the line. The night you came back from the icecap, the night she was really certain for the first time that Arnie had made a fool of her, she brought me out here to the barn. I thought it was just for a tumble in the hay, but there was more to it than that—a lot more. If I could squeeze the emeralds out of Arnie we could split them fifty-fifty and clear out in my boat."

God knows why, but it was as if I had known all along and my voice when I spoke, seemed to belong to someone else.

"Why did you kill him?"

"I didn't mean to. I knew he couldn't very well go running to the police. I was going to give him something to keep him happy. I was holding him with his own shotgun and he tried to jump me. It was as simple as that."

Sarah Kelso shook her head. "But it isn't possible."

Desforge shrugged. "What she's trying to tell you is that we were in bed together when it happened."

"That was certainly my impression," I said.

He turned to Sarah Kelso. "Sorry, angel, but I left you for an hour. That's all it took. You were sleeping like a baby."

"You fool," I said. "You stupid bloody fool. Now what happens? What *can* happen?"

"Christ knows, it's a mess." He shook his head. "I never thought it would end up like this. In the beginning it seemed like a good idea. I was desperate. There was nothing left, Joe. That letter from Milt was a death sentence. There was a court order out on my property in California against back taxes and the picture deal had fallen through. I was finished. Have you any idea what that meant? There was nothing to come. There was never going to be another picture."

It was as if he was talking for me alone, as if I was the only person there and in a strange way I understood what he was trying to say. He wasn't making excuses—he was just trying to get me to understand. All his life he's inhabited the fantasy world, living a series of incredible adventures each contained in its own watertight compartment and as one finished, another began. If you made a mistake the director shouted *Cut* and you tried it again. Nothing was for real—nothing was ever for real and suddenly, I realised what he must have felt like after killing Arnie, standing there with the noise of the shotgun still ringing in his ears, looking down on his handiwork and realising with horror, that this was permanent, this was something that couldn't be adjusted ever.

Ilana stared at him mutely, a kind of dazed incomprehension in her eyes. He ignored her and said to Vogel, "It seems to me you and I have something in common after all. How were you hoping to get away from here? By rendezvousing with Da Gama's schooner?"

Vogel shook his head. "You're wasting your time, I've no room for passengers."

"You're living in cloud-cuckoo land. Tell him, Joe."

I nodded. "He's right. Even if the schooner makes it in one piece, there's a Danish corvette doing coastal survey work out of Godthaab that could run you down in half a day."

Vogel turned back to Desforge, a slight frown on his

face. "You have something else on your mind or you would not have raised the matter."

Desforge lit a cigarette. "There's always the Otter down there in the fjord."

For the first time Vogel's iron composure cracked and he clutched at what was, after all, the only real hope of extricating himself from what was an otherwise impossible situation.

"You can fly?"

"Not like laughing boy here, but good enough for short hauls. Newfoundland, for instance."

"We could reach Newfoundland?"

"Easily with what's in the tank now. Plenty of remote fishing villages where we could put down and pick up enough gas to continue. We could make somewhere like Maine for our second landing. I'm willing to take my chances after that. America is a big country. Of course I'd expect a cut in the emeralds. Fifty per cent would seem to be about right."

I could almost see Vogel's brain working as he decided that he could handle that one at the right time and place. "Agreed. Is there anything else?"

Desforge held out his hand. "I think I'd like to look after the bank if you don't mind. After all, you and bully boy here seem to be carrying all the artillery."

Vogel hesitated fractionally and probably decided there was no harm in humouring him. He tossed the belt across. Desforge folded it neatly and stuffed it inside his parka.

"Another thing, no more trouble." He nodded towards Da Gama. "I don't want Frankenstein there cutting loose on my friends or anything like that. Now tell him to get the Landrover."

"Just as you say, Mr. Desforge."

Ilana turned and hurried away and he had to run to

catch her at the door. She started to struggle and he
held her very firmly and then she seemed to go limp
and sagged against the wall. He had his back to us, hiding her from view and it was impossible to hear what
he said, but when Da Gama drove the Landrover into
the yard, he turned and came back towards us and I
saw that Ilana was crying bitterly.

As Desforge approached, I moved into his path.
"You're kidding yourself," I said. "Even if our friend
here doesn't put a bullet through your head at the
appropriate time, where on this earth can Jack Desforge
hope to hide and not be recognised?"

He laughed. "You've got a point there, kid, but there
must be somewhere. I'll have to think about it."

As Vogel climbed into the Landrover, Sarah Kelso
said something to him in a low voice. He pushed her
away angrily. "You've made your bed—now lie on it."

She turned on Desforge, desperation on her face.
"For God's sake, Jack, if I ever meant anything to you,
take me with you. He says I can't go."

Desforge laughed incredulously. "You've got your
nerve, angel, I'll say that for you. Go on, get in! I'd say
we just about deserve each other."

He turned to me and smiled sombrely. "Strange how
things work out. Have you ever wondered how many
changes you'd make in your life if you could do the
whole thing over again?"

"Often," I said.

"Me too." He nodded. "But I'd only need to make
one. Remember the pier at Santa Barbara in the fog
when I met Lilian Courtney for the first time? I should
have turned and run like hell."

It was an interesting thought, but there was no time
to take it any further. He got into the passenger seat
beside Da Gama and turned and looked at me for the

last time. For a second, there was something there, an unspoken message that I couldn't hope to understand and he smiled that famous smile of his, sardonic and bitter, touching something deep inside me, the old indefinable magic that had moved millions of people through the years in exactly the same way.

And then he was gone, the Landrover disappearing into the rain with a roar. When I turned, Ilana had sunk down on her knees beside the door, leaning against the wall, crying steadily.

I went forward and took her by the elbow. Her sheepskin coat was unbuttoned for some reason and as I pulled her up, it opened and the money belt fell to the ground.

I stared down at it in stupefaction, then picked it up awkwardly with my left hand. "What's this?" I said hoarsely.

"The emeralds," she said. "Don't you understand? He slipped them under my coat when he was saying goodbye."

Perhaps I had lost more blood than I realised or maybe I was moving into shock, but suddenly nothing seemed to make too much sense any more.

I shook my head as if to clear my sight and said carefully, "But why would he do that? What on earth could he hope to accomplish?"

And then it hit me with the force of a thunderbolt, and I realised what his eyes had been trying to say in those last moments before the Landrover had driven away into the fog. When I looked up, Ilana was staring at me in horror as if she too had suddenly discovered the only possible explanation.

She shook her head dumbly and I pushed the belt inside my flying jacket and grabbed her arm. "The jeep —where is it?"

"Somewhere behind the barn."

I turned and ran and heard her call through the rain. "Don't leave me, Joe! Don't leave me!" There was panic in her voice.

I found the jeep, just as she had said, but with one difference. It was standing in a lake of petrol, a bullet hole in the tank and I turned, ignoring her desperate cry, scrambled over the wall and ran through the meadow.

I was wasting my time, I suppose I knew that from the start and yet nothing in this world could have stopped me. I clambered over the fence at the bottom of the meadow and as I went down the slope through the willow trees, the engine of the Otter coughed angrily in the rain below and roared into life.

As I reached the top of the crag, the Otter roared down the fjord, the engine note deepening so that I knew she was lifting off. There was a sudden crashing through the trees behind me as Ilana arrived and at the same moment, a wind coming down from the icecap swept the rain to one side like a giant curtain and I saw the Otter for the last time, five hundred feet up and climbing into the morning.

And then she turned, as I knew she would, and came back across the fjord, heading straight for that great wall of stone and going like a bomb.

God knows what happened in that cabin during those last few minutes. I suppose Vogel must have emptied his gun into him, but he held her on the course of his own choosing, straight and true, Jack Desforge, that magnificent, wonderful bastard going out as he had lived in a blaze of glory.

The explosion echoed between the hills as a ball of fire erupted against the side of the mountain and then mercifully, the wind died and the curtain of rain dropped back into place.

*

I think that at that moment I could have sat down and wept for him and for the cruel, senseless waste of it all, but there was no time for that now. Ilana stood staring into the void, then turned and stumbled towards me, tears streaming down her face. I pulled her against my chest and stroked her hair with my one good hand.

"Why did he do it, Joe? Why?" she said brokenly.

I could have given her the obvious answer. That he was tired, that he'd had enough, that he knew, as I had told him, that there was no place on earth for him to hide, but I could do better for him than that.

"To save us," I said. "He agreed to fly Vogel out to save us and for no other reason. But somewhere along the line he was going to get a bullet in the head, he knew that. He decided to take them with him, that's all. There isn't a newspaper or magazine in the world that won't swallow that hook line and sinker. They'll believe it because they want to believe it."

"And Arnie? What about Arnie?"

"Vogel and Stratton killed Arnie," I said patiently. "I thought you knew that."

She stood there staring at me, a hand to her mouth and I patted her on the shoulder and said gently, "Now go back to the farmhouse like a good girl. I'll be along later." She hesitated and I gave her a push. "Go on."

She stared up through the grove and I watched her go. She paused at the edge of the trees and turned. "You won't leave me, Joe?"

"No, I won't leave you, Ilana."

I waited till she had gone then scrambled over the edge of the crag and slowly and painfully made my way down to the beach. Whichever way you looked at it, it was ironic. By this time next year somebody would probably be sinking a million or so into a film of it all. I wondered who they'd get to play me and suddenly the whole thing seemed so ludicrous that I started to laugh and the sound of it echoed back across the water as if Desforge was laughing with me.

I found the horseshoe of black rocks on the beach where I had hidden from Stratton earlier with no difficulty and slumped down wearily. What happened to me now didn't seem to matter. After all, what could they do? Probably a deportation order and maybe I'd lose my licence, but both these things seemed relatively trivial.

One thing was certain. Nothing must be allowed to diminish the magnificence of that final sacrifice. I took the money belt from inside my flying jacket, opened the pouches one by one and emptied them of the pebbles they contained.

The emeralds were where I had left them in a little pile under a flat stone. Slowly and with great difficulty because I could only use my left hand, I started to replace them.

LUCIANO'S LUCK

1943. Under cover of night, a strange group parachutes into Nazi occupied Sicily. It includes the overlord of the American Mafia, "Lucky" Luciano. The object? To convince the Sicilian Mafia king to put his power—the power of the Sicilian peasantry—behind the invading American forces. It is a dangerous gamble. If they fail, hundreds of thousands will die on Sicilian soil. If they succeed, American troops will march through Sicily toward a stunning victory on the Italian Front, forever indebted to Mafia king, Lucky Luciano.

A DELL BOOK   14321-7 $3.50

JACK HIGGINS

bestselling author of *Solo*

MORE
GREAT READING
FROM

Robert B. Parker

the author of Ceremony

"Robert B. Parker
has taken his place
beside Dashiell Hammett,
Raymond Chandler, and Ross
MacDonald."—*The Boston Globe*

"Crackling dialogue, plenty of action and
expert writing."—*The New York Times*

"Truly hard to put down."—*Newsday*

Looking for
Rachel Wallace	$2.50	15316-6
Early Autumn	$2.50	12214-7
A Savage Place	$2.95	18095-3
Wilderness	$2.25	19328-1

At your local bookstore or use this handy coupon for ordering:

Dell | DELL BOOKS
P.O. BOX 1000, PINE BROOK, N.J. 07058-1000

Please send me the books I have checked above. I am enclosing $_____ (please add 75¢ per copy to
cover postage and handling). Send check or money order—no cash or C.O.D.'s. Please allow up to 8 weeks for
shipment.

Mr./Mrs./Miss _____

Address _____

City _____ State/Zip _____